SWIMMING HOME

Deborah Levy writes fiction, plays and poetry. Her work has been staged by the Royal Shakespeare Company, and she is the author of highly praised books including *Beautiful Mutants*, *Swallowing Geography* (both Jonathan Cape) and *Billy and Girl* (Bloomsbury).

Further praise for *Swimming Home*:

'One of the finest new novels I have read (and already re-read) in a long time . . . It radiates the sensual languor of sun-drenched afternoons in the south of France and the disquieting, uncanny beauty only perceived by a true daytime insomniac.' Andrew Gallix, *Guardian*

'*Swimming Home* is as sharp as a wasp sting . . . Witty and poignant, [its] 165 pages melt away like an unsettling yet familiar dream.' Christina Petrie, *Sunday Times*

'Deborah Levy has made something strange and new . . . spiky and unsettling. In this novel, home is elusive, safety is unlikely, and the reader closes the book both satisfied and unnerved.' John Self, *Guardian*

'Deborah Levy's storytelling is allusive, elliptical and disturbing. Her touch is gentle, often funny and always acute. This amazing novel is a haunting exploration of loss and longing. She is also strong on suspense, leading the reader to a hugely surprising end . . . It has an epic quality. This is a prizewinner.' Julia Pascal, *Independent*

'A statement on the power of the unsaid. Magisterial . . . Themes, phrases and images recur in rhythmic cycles through this fugal novel. Levy's cinematic clarity and momentum convey confusion with remarkable lucidity.' Abigail Deutsch, *TLS*

'As the reader is drawn beneath the placid surface of her characters' experiences, Levy reveals a more urgent world humming with symbols.' Sammy Jay, *Literary Review*

SWIMMING HOME

Deborah Levy

Afterword by Tom McCarthy

faber and faber

First published in 2011 by
And Other Stories
91 Tadros Court, High Wycombe, Bucks, HP13 7GF

This paperback edition published in 2012 by And Other Stories and
Faber and Faber, Bloomsbury House, 74–77 Great Russell Street,
London WC1B 3DA

Printed and bound by CPI Group (UK) Ltd, Croydon, CR0 4YY

www.andotherstories.org

www.faber.co.uk

ISBN 978-0-571-29960-7

A catalogue record for this book is available from the British Library

Supported by the National Lottery through Arts Council England.

LOTTERY FUNDED

10 9 8 7

To Sadie and Leila, so dear, always

'Each morning in every family, men, women and children, *if they have nothing better to do*, tell each other their dreams. We are all at the mercy of the dream and we owe it to ourselves to submit its power to the waking state.'

– *La Révolution surréaliste*, No. 1, December 1924

SWIMMING HOME

ALPES-MARITIMES, FRANCE

July 1994

A Mountain Road. Midnight.

When Kitty Finch took her hand off the steering wheel and told him she loved him, he no longer knew if she was threatening him or having a conversation. Her silk dress was falling off her shoulders as she bent over the steering wheel. A rabbit ran across the road and the car swerved. He heard himself say, 'Why don't you pack a rucksack and see the poppy fields in Pakistan like you said you wanted to?'

'Yes,' she said.

He could smell petrol. Her hands swooped over the steering wheel like the seagulls they had counted from their room in the Hotel Negresco two hours ago.

She asked him to open his window so she could hear the insects calling to each other in the forest. He wound down the window and asked her, gently, to keep her eyes on the road.

'Yes,' she said again, her eyes now back on the road. And then she told him the nights were always 'soft' in the French Riviera. The days were hard and smelt of money.

He leaned his head out of the window and felt the cold mountain air sting his lips. Early humans had once lived in this forest that was now a road. They knew the past lived in rocks and trees and they knew desire made them awkward, mad, mysterious, messed up.

To have been so intimate with Kitty Finch had been a pleasure, a pain, a shock, an experiment, but most of all it had been a mistake. He asked her again to please, please, please drive him safely home to his wife and daughter.

'Yes,' she said. 'Life is only worth living because we hope it will get better and we'll all get home safely.'

SATURDAY

Wild Life

The swimming pool in the grounds of the tourist villa was more like a pond than the languid blue pools in holiday brochures. A pond in the shape of a rectangle, carved from stone by a family of Italian stonecutters living in Antibes. The body was floating near the deep end, where a line of pine trees kept the water cool in their shade.

'Is it a bear?' Joe Jacobs waved his hand vaguely in the direction of the water. He could feel the sun burning into the shirt his Hindu tailor had made for him from a roll of raw silk. His back was on fire. Even the roads were melting in the July heatwave.

His daughter, Nina Jacobs, fourteen years old, standing at the edge of the pool in her new cherry-print bikini, glanced anxiously at her mother. Isabel Jacobs was unzipping her jeans as if she was about to dive in. At the same time she could see Mitchell and Laura, the two family friends sharing the villa with them for the summer, put down their mugs of tea and walk towards the stone steps that led to the shallow end. Laura, a slender giantess at six foot three, kicked off her sandals and waded in up to her knees. A battered yellow lilo knocked against the mossy sides, scattering the bees that were in various stages of dying in the water.

'What do you think it is, Isabel?'

Nina could see from where she was standing that it was a woman swimming naked under the water. She was on her stomach, both arms stretched out like a starfish, her long hair floating like seaweed at the sides of her body.

'Jozef thinks she's a bear,' Isabel Jacobs replied in her detached war-correspondent voice.

'If it's a bear I'm going to have to shoot it.' Mitchell had recently purchased two antique Persian handguns at the flea market in Nice and shooting things was on his mind.

Yesterday they had all been discussing a newspaper article about a ninety-four-kilo bear that had walked down from the mountains in Los Angeles and taken a dip in a Hollywood actor's pool. The bear was on heat, according to the Los Angeles Animal Services. The actor had called the authorities. The bear was shot with a tranquilliser gun and then released in the nearby mountains. Joe Jacobs had wondered out loud what it was like to be tranquillised and then have to stumble home. Did it ever get home? Did it get dizzy and forgetful and start to hallucinate? Perhaps the barbiturate inserted inside the dart, also known as 'chemical capture', had made the bear's legs shake and jerk? Had the tranquilliser helped the bear cope with life's stressful events, calming its agitated mind so that it now pleaded with the authorities to throw it small prey injected with barbiturate syrups? Joe had only stopped this riff when Mitchell stood on his toe. As far as Mitchell was concerned it was very, very hard to get the arsehole poet known to his readers as JHJ (Joe to every one else except his wife) to shut the fuck up.

Nina watched her mother dive into the murky green water and swim towards the woman. Saving the lives of bloated bodies floating in rivers was probably the sort of thing her mother did all the time. Apparently television ratings always went up when she was on the news. Her mother disappeared to Northern Ireland and Lebanon and Kuwait and then she came back as if she'd just nipped down the road to buy a pint of milk. Isabel Jacobs' hand was about to clasp the ankle of whoever it was floating in the pool. A sudden violent splash made Nina run to her father, who grasped her sunburnt shoulder, making her scream out loud. When a head emerged from the water, its mouth open and gasping for breath, for one panicked second she thought it was roaring like a bear.

A woman with dripping waist-length hair climbed out of the pool and ran to one of the plastic recliners. She looked like she might be in her early twenties, but it was hard to tell because she was frantically skipping from one chair to another, searching for her dress. It had fallen on to the paving stones but no one helped her because they were staring at her naked body. Nina felt light-headed in the fierce heat. The bittersweet smell of lavender drifted towards her, suffocating her as the sound of the woman's panting breath mingled with the drone of the bees in the wilting flowers. It occurred to her she might be sun-sick, because she felt as if she was going to faint. In a blur she could see the woman's breasts were surprisingly full and round for someone so thin. Her long thighs were joined to the jutting hinges of her hips like the legs of the dolls she used to bend and twist as a child. The only thing that seemed real about the woman was the triangle of golden pubic hair glinting in the sun. The sight of it made Nina fold her arms across her chest and hunch her back in an effort to make her own body disappear.

'Your dress is over there.' Joe Jacobs pointed to the pile of crumpled blue cotton lying under the recliner. They had all been staring at her for an embarrassingly long time. The woman grabbed it and deftly slipped the flimsy dress over her head.

'Thanks. I'm Kitty Finch by the way.'

What she actually said was I'm Kah Kah Kah and stammered on for ever until she got to Kitty Finch. Everyone couldn't wait for her to finish saying who she was.

Nina realised her mother was still in the pool. When she climbed up the stone steps, her wet swimming costume was covered in silver pine needles.

'I'm Isabel. My husband thought you were a bear.'

Joe Jacobs twisted his lips in an effort not to laugh.

'Of course I didn't think she was a bear.'

Kitty Finch's eyes were grey like the tinted windows of Mitchell's hire car, a Mercedes, parked on the gravel at the front of the villa.

'I hope you don't mind me using the pool. I've just

arrived and it's sooo hot. There's been a mistake with the rental dates.'

'What sort of mistake?' Laura glared at the young woman as if she had just been handed a parking ticket.

'Well, I thought I was staying here from this Saturday for a fortnight. But the caretaker . . .'

'If you can call a lazy stoned bastard like Jurgen a caretaker.' Just mentioning Jurgen's name brought Mitchell out in a disgusted sweat.

'Yeah. Jurgen says I've got the dates all wrong and now I'm going to lose my deposit.'

Jurgen was a German hippy who was never exact about anything. He described himself as 'a nature man' and always had his nose buried in *Siddhartha* by Hermann Hesse.

Mitchell wagged his finger at her. 'There are worse things than losing your deposit. We were about to have you sedated and driven up to the mountains.'

Kitty Finch lifted up the sole of her left foot and slowly pulled out a thorn. Her grey eyes searched for Nina, who was still hiding behind her father. And then she smiled.

'I like your bikini.' Her front teeth were crooked, snarled into each other, and her hair was drying into copper-coloured curls. 'What's your name?'

'Nina.'

'Do you think I look like a bear, Nina?' She clenched her right hand as if it was a paw and jabbed it at the cloudless blue sky. Her fingernails were painted dark green.

Nina shook her head and then swallowed her spit the wrong way and started to cough. Everyone sat down. Mitchell on the ugly blue chair because he was the fattest and it was the biggest, Laura on the pink wicker chair, Isabel and Joe on the two white plastic recliners. Nina perched on the edge of her father's chair and fiddled with the five silver toe-rings Jurgen had given her that morning. They all had a place in the shade except Kitty Finch, who was crouching awkwardly on the burning paving stones.

'You haven't anywhere to sit. I'll find you a chair.' Isabel wrung the ends of her wet black hair. Drops of water glistened on her shoulders and then ran down her arm like a snake.

Kitty shook her head and blushed. 'Oh, don't bother. Pah pah please. I'm just waiting for Jurgen to come back with the name of a hotel for me and I'll be off.'

'Of course you must sit down.'

Laura, puzzled and uneasy, watched Isabel lug a heavy wooden chair covered in dust and cobwebs towards the pool. There were things in the way. A red bucket. A broken plant pot. Two canvas umbrellas wedged into lumps of concrete. No one helped her because they weren't quite sure what she was doing. Isabel, who had somehow managed to pin up her wet hair with a clip in the shape of a lily, was actually placing the wooden chair between her recliner and her husband's.

Kitty Finch glanced nervously at Isabel and then at Joe, as if she couldn't work out if she was being offered the chair or being forced to sit in it. She wiped away the cobwebs with the skirt of her dress for much too long and then finally sat down. Laura folded her hands in her lap as if preparing to interview an applicant for a job.

'Have you been here before?'

'Yes. I've been coming here for years.'

'Do you work?' Mitchell spat an olive pip into a bowl.

'I sort of work. I'm a botanist.'

Joe stroked the small shaving cut on his chin and smiled at her. 'There are some nice peculiar words in your profession.'

His voice was surprisingly gentle, as if he intuited Kitty Finch was offended by the way Laura and Mitchell were interrogating her.

'Yeah. Joe likes pe-cu-li-ar words cos he's a poet.' Mitchell said 'peculiar' as if imitating an aristocrat in a stupor.

Joe leaned back in his chair and closed his eyes. 'Ignore him, Kitty.' He sounded as if he had been wounded in some inexplicable way. 'Everything is pe-cu-li-ar to Mitchell. Strangely enough, this makes him feel superior.'

Mitchell stuffed five olives into his mouth one after the other and then spat out the pips in Joe's direction as if they were little bullets from one of his minor guns.

'So in the meantime ' – Joe leaned forward now – 'perhaps you could tell us what you know about cotyledons?'

'Right.' Kitty's right eye winked at Nina when she said 'right'. 'Cotyledons are the first leaves on a seedling.' Her stammer seemed to have disappeared.

'Correct. And now for my favourite word . . . how would you describe a leaf?'

'Kitty,' Laura said sternly, 'there are lots of hotels, so you'd better go and find one.'

When Jurgen finally made his way through the gate, his silver dreadlocks tied back in a ponytail, he told them every hotel in the village was full until Thursday.

'Then you must stay until Thursday.' Isabel said this vaguely, as if she didn't quite believe it. 'I think there's a spare room at the back of the house.'

Kitty frowned and leaned back in her new chair.

'Well, yeah. Thanks. Is that OK with everyone else? Please say if you mind.'

It seemed to Nina that she was asking them to mind. Kitty Finch was blushing and clenching her toes at the same time. Nina felt her own heart racing. It had gone hysterical, thumping in her chest. She glanced at Laura and saw she was actually wringing her hands. Laura was about to say she did mind. She and Mitchell had shut their shop in Euston for the entire summer, knowing the windows that had been smashed by thieves and drug addicts at least three times that year would be smashed again when their holiday was over. They had come to the Alpes-Maritimes to escape from the futility of mending broken glass. She found herself struggling for words. The young woman was a window waiting to be climbed through. A window that she guessed was a little broken anyway. She couldn't be sure of this, but it seemed to her that Joe Jacobs had already wedged his foot into the crack and his wife had helped him. She cleared her throat and was about to speak her mind, but what was on her mind was so unutterable the hippy caretaker got there first.

'So, Kitty Ket, shall I carry your valises to your room?'

Everyone looked to where Jurgen was pointing with his nicotine-stained finger. Two blue canvas bags lay to the right of the French doors of the villa.

'Thanks, Jurgen.' Kitty dismissed him as if he was her personal valet.

He bent down and picked up the bags.

'What are the weeds?' He lifted up a tangle of flowering plants that had been stuffed into the second blue bag.

'Oh, I found those in the churchyard next to Claude's café.'

Jurgen looked impressed.

'You'll have to call them the Kitty Ket plant. It is a historical fact. Plant hunters often named the plants they found after themselves.'

'Yeah.' She stared past him in to Joe Jacobs' dark eyes as if to say, 'Jurgen's special name for me is Kitty Ket.'

Isabel walked to the edge of the pool and dived in. As she swam low under the water, her arms stretched out in front of her head, she saw her watch lying on the bottom of the pool. She flipped over and scooped it up from the green tiles. When she surfaced she saw the old English woman who lived next door waving from her balcony. She waved back and then realised Madeleine Sheridan was waving to Mitchell, who was calling out her name.

Interpreting a Smile

'Madel-eeene!'

It was the fat man who liked guns calling up to her. Madeleine Sheridan lifted up her arthritic arm and waved with two limp fingers from her straw chair. Her body had become a sum of flawed parts. At medical school she had learned she had twenty-seven bones in each hand, eight in the wrist alone, five in the palm. Her fingers were rich in nerve endings but now even moving two fingers was an effort.

She wanted to remind Jurgen, whom she could see carrying Kitty Finch's bags into the villa, that it was her birthday in six days' time, but she was reluctant to appear so begging of his company in front of the English tourists. Perhaps she was dead already and had been watching the drama of the young woman's arrival from the Other Side? Four months ago, in March, when Kitty Finch was staying alone at the tourist villa (apparently to study mountain plants), she had informed Madeleine Sheridan that a breeze would help her tomatoes grow stronger stems and offered to thin the leaves for her. This she proceeded to do, but she was whispering to herself all the while, pah pah pah, kah kah kah, consonants that made hard sounds on her lips. Madeleine Sheridan, who believed human beings had to suffer real hardships before they agreed to lose their minds, told her in a steely voice to stop making that noise. To stop it. To stop it right now. Today was Saturday and the noise had come back to France to haunt her. It had even been offered a room in the villa.

•

'Madel-eeene, I'm cooking beef tonight. Why don't you join us for supper?'

She could just make out the pink dome of Mitchell's balding head as she squinted at him in the sun. Madeleine Sheridan, who was quite partial to beef and often lonely in the evenings, wondered if she had it in herself to decline Mitchell's invitation. She thought she did. When couples offer shelter or a meal to strays and loners, they do not really take them in. They play with them. Perform for them. And when they are done they tell their stranded guest in all sorts of sly ways she is now required to leave. Couples were always keen to return to the task of trying to destroy their lifelong partners while pretending to have their best interests at heart. A single guest was a mere distraction from this task.

'Madel-eeene.'

Mitchell seemed more anxious than usual. Yesterday he told her he had spotted Keith Richards drinking Pepsi in Villefranche-sur-Mer and was desperate to ask for his autograph. In the end he didn't because, in his own words, 'The arsehole poet was with me and threatened to headbutt me for being normal.'

Mitchell with his flabby, prawn-pink arms amused her when he gloomily observed that Joe Jacobs was not the sort of poet who gazed at the moon and had no muscle tone. He could probably lift a wardrobe with his teeth. Especially if it had a beautiful woman inside it. When the English tourists arrived two weeks ago, Joe Jacobs (JHJ on his books but she'd

15

never heard of him) knocked on her door to borrow some salt. He was wearing a winter suit on the hottest day of the year and when she pointed this out, he told her it was his sister's birthday and he always wore a suit to show his respect.

This bemused her, because her own birthday was much on her mind. His suit seemed more appropriate for a funeral but he was so charming and attentive she asked him if he would like to try the Andalucían almond soup she had made earlier. When he muttered, 'How kind, my dear,' she poured a generous amount into one of her favourite ceramic bowls and invited him to drink it on her balcony. Something terrible happened. He took a sip and felt something tangle with his teeth, only to discover it was her hair. A small clump of silver hair had somehow found its way into the bowl. He was mortified beyond her comprehension, even though she apologised, unable to fathom how it had got there. His hands were actually shaking and he pushed the bowl away with such force the soup spilt all over his ridiculous pinstriped suit, its jacket lined with dandyish pink silk. She thought a poet might have done better than that. He could have said, 'Your soup was like drinking a cloud.'

'Madel-eeene.'

Mitchell couldn't even say her name properly. Possibly because he had such a ridiculous name himself. The prospect of having to live with Kitty Finch had obviously got him into a panic and she wasn't surprised. She squeezed her eyes into slits, enjoying the view of her ugly bare feet. It was such a pleasure not to wear socks and shoes. Even after fifteen years living in France, wrenched as she was from her country of birth and her first language, it was the pleasure of naked feet she was most grateful for. She could live without a slice of Mitchell's succulent beef. And she would be insanely brave to risk an evening in the company of Kitty Finch, who was pretending not to have seen her. Right now she was scooping pine cones out of the pool with Nina Jacobs as if her life depended on it. There was no way Madeleine Sheridan, six days away from turning eighty, would perform like a dignified old woman at the dinner table in the tourist villa. The same table Jurgen had bought at the flea market and polished with beeswax and paraffin. What's more, he had polished it in his underpants because of the heatwave. She had had to avert her eyes at the sight of him sweating in what she delicately called his 'undergarments'.

An eagle was hovering in the sky. It had seen the mice that ran through the uncut grass in the orchard.

She called down her excuses to Mitchell, but he seemed not to have heard her. He was watching Joe Jacobs disappear inside the villa to find a hat. Kitty Finch was apparently going to take the English poet for a walk and show him some flowers. Madeleine Sheridan couldn't be sure of this, but she thought the mad girl with her halo of red hair shining in the sun might be smiling at her.

To use the language of a war correspondent, which was, she knew, what Isabel Jacobs happened to be, she would have to say that Kitty Finch was smiling at her with hostile intent.

The Botany Lesson

There were signs everywhere saying the orchard was private property, but Kitty insisted she knew the farmer and no one was going to set the dogs on them. For the last twenty minutes she had been pointing out trees that, in her view, 'were not doing too well'.

'Do you only notice trees that suffer?' Joe Jacobs shaded his eyes with his hands, which were covered in mosquito bites, and stared into her bright grey eyes.

'Yes, I suppose I do.'

He was convinced he could hear an animal growling in the grass and told her it sounded like a dog.

'Don't worry about the dogs. The farmer owns 2,000 olive trees in the Grasse area. He's too busy to set his dogs on us.'

'Well, I suppose that many olive trees would keep him busy,' Joe mumbled.

His black hair now fading into silver curls fell in a mess around his ears and the battered straw hat kept slipping off his head. Kitty had to run behind him to pick it up.

'Oh, 2,000 . . . that's not a lot of trees . . . not at all.'

She stooped down to peer at wild flowers growing between the long white grasses that came up to her knees.

'These are *Bellis perennis*.' She scooped up what looked like daisy petals and stuffed them in her mouth. 'Plants are always from some sort of family.'

She buried her face in the flowers she was clutching and named them for him in Latin. He was impressed by the tender way she held the plants in her fingers and spoke about them with easy intimacy, as if indeed they were a family with various problems and unusual qualities. And then she told him what she wanted most in life was to see the poppy fields in Pakistan.

'Actually,' she confessed nervously, 'I've written a poem about that.'

Joe stopped walking. So that was why she was here.

Young women who followed him about and wanted him to read their poetry, and he was now convinced she was one of them, always started by telling him they'd written a poem about something extraordinary. They walked side by side, flattening a path through the long grass. He waited for her to speak, to make her request, to say how influenced by his books she was, to explain how she'd managed to track him down, and then she would ask would he mind, did he have time, would he be so kind as to please, please read her small effort inspired by himself.

'So you've read all my books and now you've followed me to France,' he said sharply.

A new wave of blush crashed over her cheeks and long neck.

'Yes. Rita Dwighter, who owns the villa, is a friend of my mother. Rita told me you had booked it for the whole summer. She lets me stay in her house for free off-season. I couldn't stay because YOU hah hah hah hah hogged it.'

'But it's not off-season, Kitty. July is what they call the high season, isn't it?'

She had a north London accent. Her front teeth were

crooked. When she wasn't stammering and blushing she looked like she'd been sculpted from wax in a dark workshop in Venice. If she was a botanist she obviously did not spend much time outside. Whoever had made her was clever. She could swim and cry and blush and say things like 'hogged it'.

'Let's sit in the shade.'

He pointed to a large tree surrounded by small rocks. A plump brown pigeon perched comically on a thin branch that looked like it was about to snap under its weight.

'All right. That's a haaaah hazelnut tree by the way.'

He charged ahead before she finished her sentence and sat down, leaning his back against the tree trunk. When she seemed reluctant to join him he patted the space next to him, brushing away the twigs and leaves until she sat down by his side, smoothing her faded blue cotton dress over her knees. He could not so much hear her heart as feel it beating under her thin dress.

'When I write poems I always think you can hear them.'

A bell tinkled in the distance. It sounded like a goat grazing somewhere in the orchard, moving around in the long grass.

'Why are you shaking?' He could smell chlorine in her hair.

'Yeah. I've stopped taking my pills so my hands are a bit shaky.'

Kitty moved a little nearer him. He wasn't too sure what to make of this until he saw she was avoiding a line of red ants crawling under her calves.

'Why do you take pills?'

'Oh, I've decided not to for a while. You know . . . it's quite a relief to feel miserable again. I don't feel anything when I take my pills.'

She slapped at the ants crawling over her ankles.

'I wrote about that too . . . it's called "Picking Roses on Seroxat".'

Joe fumbled for a scrap of green silk in his pocket and blew his nose. 'What's Seroxat?'

'You know what it is.'

His nose was buried in the silk handkerchief.

'Tell me anyway,' he snuffled.

'Seroxat is a really strong antidepressant. I've been on it for years.'

Kitty stared at the sky smashing against the mountains. He found himself reaching for her cold shaking hand and held it tight in his lap. She was right to be indignant at his question. Clasping her hand was a silent acknowledgement that he knew she had read him because he had told his readers all about his teenage years on medication. When he was fifteen he had very lightly grazed his left wrist with a razor blade. Nothing serious. Just an experiment. The blade was cool and sharp. His wrist was warm and soft. They were not supposed to be paired together but it was a teenage game of Snap. He had snapped. The doctor, an old Hungarian man with hair in his ears, had not agreed this pairing was an everyday error. He had asked questions. Biography is what the Hungarian doctor wanted.

Names and places and dates. The names of his mother, his father, his sister. The languages they spoke and how old was he when he last saw them? Joe Jacobs had replied by fainting in the consulting room and so his teenage years had been tranquillised into a one-season pharmaceutical mist. Or as he had suggested in his most famous poem, now translated into twenty-three languages: a bad fairy made a deal with me, 'give me your history and I will give you something to take it away'.

When he turned to look at her face, now drained of its blush, her cheeks were wet.

'Why are you crying?'

'I'm OK.' Her voice was matter of fact.

'I'm pleased to save money and not spend it on a hotel, but I didn't expect your wife to offer me the spare room.'

Three black flies settled on his forehead, but he did not let go of her hand to flick them away. He passed her the scrap of silk he kept as a handkerchief.

'Mop yourself up.'

'I don't want your handkerchief.' She threw the scrap of silk back into his lap. 'And I hate it when people say mop yourself up. Like I'm a dirty floor.'

He couldn't be sure of it, but he thought that was a line from one of his poems too. Not quite as it was written but near enough. He noticed a scratch running across her left ankle and she told him it was where his wife had grabbed her foot in the pool.

The goat was getting nearer. Every time it moved the bell rang. When it was still the bell stopped. It made him feel uneasy. He brushed a small green cricket off his shoulder and placed it in her open palm.

'I think you've written something you'd like me to read. Is that right?'

'Yes. It's just one poem.' Again her voice was matter of fact. She set the cricket free, watching it jump into the grass and disappear. 'It's a conversation with you, really.'

Joe picked up a twig that had fallen from the tree. The brown pigeon above his head was chancing its luck. There were stronger branches it could move to but it refused to budge. He told her he would read her poem that evening and waited for her to thank him.

He waited. For her thank-yous. For his time. For his attention. For his generosity. For defending her against Mitchell. For his company and for his words, the poetry that had made her more or less stalk him on a family holiday. Her thank-yous did not arrive.

'By the way' – he stared at her pale shins covered in crushed ants – 'the fact I know that you um take medication and all that . . . is confidential.'

She shrugged. 'Well, actually, Jurgen and Dr Sheridan and everyone in the village know already. And I've stopped taking it anyway.'

'Is Madeleine Sheridan a doctor?'

'Yeah.' She clenched her toes. 'She's got friends at the hospital in Grasse, so you'd better pretend to be happy and have a grip.'

He laughed and then to make him laugh some more, so he would appear to be happy and to have a grip, she advised him that nothing, NOTHING AT ALL, was confidential when it was told to Jurgen. 'Like all indiscreet people, he puts his hand on his heart and assures his confidant that his lips are sealed. Jurgen's lips are never sealed, because they always have a giant spliff between them.'

Joe Jacobs knew he should ask her more questions. Like his journalist wife. The why the how the when the who and all the other words he was supposed to ask to make life more coherent. But she had given him a little information. On the way to the orchard she told him she had given up her job clearing leaves and cutting grass in Victoria Park in Hackney. A gang of boys had pulled a knife on her because when she was on medication it made her legs twitch so she was easy prey.

They heard the bell again.

'What is it?' Kitty stood up and peered into the long grass.

Joe could see the vertebrae of her spine under her dress. When he dropped his hat once again, she picked it up and dusted it with the tips of her green fingernails, holding it out to him.

'Oh!'

Kitty shouted 'Oh' because at that moment the long grass moved and they saw flashes of pink and silver glinting through the blades. Something was making its way towards them. The grass seemed to open and Nina stood in front of them, barefoot in her cherry-print bikini. On her toes were Jurgen's gift of the five silver rings from India with little bells attached to them.

'I came to find you.' She gazed at her father, who seemed to be holding Kitty's Finch's hand. 'Mum's gone to Nice. She said she had to take her shoes to get mended.'

24

Kitty looked at the watch on her thin wrist.

'But the cobblers are shut in Nice now.'

Three growling dogs sprang out of the grass and circled them. When the farmer appeared and told the sweating English poet that he was trespassing on his land, the beautiful English girl ripped the scarf off the hat she was wearing and passed it to the frowning poet.

'Mop yourself up,' she said, and told the farmer in French to call the dogs off them.

When they got back to the villa, Joe walked through the cypress trees to the garden, where he had set up a table and chair to write in the shade. For the last two weeks he had referred to it as his study and it was understood he must not be disturbed, even when he fell asleep on the chair. Through the gaps in the branches of the cypress trees he saw Laura sitting on the faded wicker chair by the pool. Mitchell was carrying a bowl of strawberries towards her.

He glanced drowsily at Laura and Mitchell eating their strawberries in the sunshine and found himself about to fall asleep. It was an odd sensation, 'to find himself' about to fall into sleep. As if he could find himself anywhere at any time. Best to make the anywhere a good place to be, then, a place without anguish or impending threat; sitting at a table under the shade of an old tree with his family; taking photographs in a gondola moving across the canals of Venice; watching a film in an empty cinema with a can of lager between his knees. In a car on a mountain road at midnight after making love to Kitty Finch.

A Mountain Road. Midnight.

It was getting dark and she told him the brakes on the hire car were fucked, she couldn't see a thing, she couldn't even see her hands.

Her silk dress was falling off her shoulders as she bent over the steering wheel. A rabbit ran across the road and the car swerved. He told her to keep her eyes on the road, to just do that, and while he was speaking she was kissing him and driving at the same time. And then she asked him to open his window so she could hear the insects calling to each other in the forest. He wound down the window and told her, again, to keep her eyes on the road. He leaned his head out of the window and felt the cold mountain air sting his lips. Early humans had once lived in this mountain forest. They knew the past lived in rocks and trees and they knew desire made them awkward, mad, mysterious, messed up.

'Yes,' Kitty Finch said, her eyes now back on the road. 'I know what you're thinking. Life is only worth living because we hope it will get better and we'll all get home safely. But you tried and you did not get home safely. You did not get home at all. That is why I am here, Jozef. I have come to France to save you from your thoughts.'

26

Imitations of Life

Isabel Jacobs was not sure why she had lied about taking her shoes to be mended. It was just one more thing she was not sure of. After Kitty Finch's arrival all she could do to get through the day was to imitate someone she used to be, but who that was, who she used to be, no longer seemed to be a person worth imitating. The world had become increasingly mysterious. And so had she. She was not sure what she felt about anything any more, or how she felt it, or why she had offered a stranger the spare room. By the time she had driven down the mountains, found change for the toll, got lost in Vence and tried to turn back in the traffic that choked the coast road to Nice, enraged drivers jerked their hands at her, pressed their horns, rolled down their windows and shouted at her. In the back seats of their cars, groomed little dogs stared at her mockingly, as if not knowing where you were going in a one-way system was something they despised too.

She parked opposite the beach called Opéra Plage and walked towards the pink dome of the Hotel Negresco, which she recognised from the map stapled on to the 'fact sheet' that came with the villa. The fact sheet was full of information about the Hotel Negresco, the oldest and grandest belle époque hotel on the Promenade des Anglais. Apparently it was built in 1912 by Henri Negresco, a Hungarian immigrant who designed it to attract to Nice 'the very top of the upper crust'.

A breeze was blowing across the two lanes of traffic that separated her from the crowded beaches. This blast of dirty city life felt better, far better than the clean sharp mountain air that only seemed to make sorrow sharper too. Here in Nice, France's fifth biggest city, she could disappear into the crowds of holidaymakers as if she had nothing on her mind except to complain about the cost of hiring a sun lounger on the Riviera.

A woman with a helmet of permed, hennaed hair stopped her to ask if she knew the way to Rue François Aune. The lenses of her big sunglasses were smeared with what looked like dried milk. She spoke in English with an accent that Isabel thought might be Russian. The woman pointed a finger laden with rings at a mechanic in oily navy overalls lying under a motorbike, as if to suggest Isabel ask him for directions on her behalf. For a moment she couldn't work out why this was demanded of her, but then she realised the woman was blind and could hear the mechanic revving his bike nearby.

When Isabel knelt down on the pavement and showed him the scrap of paper the woman had pushed into her hand, he jerked his thumb at the apartment block across the road. The blind woman was standing in the street she was looking for. 'You are here.' Isabel took her arm and led her through the gate towards the affluent mansion block, every window framed with newly painted green shutters. Three sprinklers watered the palm trees planted in neat lines in the communal gardens.

'But I want the port, Madame. I am looking for Dr Ortega.'

The blind Russian woman sounded indignant, as if she

had been taken to the wrong place against her will. Isabel gazed at the names of residents carved on to brass plaques by the door and read them out loud: 'Perez, Orsi, Bergel, Dr Ortega.' There was his name. This was where he lived, even though the woman disagreed.

She pressed the bell for Dr Ortega and ignored the Russian woman, who was now fumbling urgently in her crocodile-skin handbag for what turned out to be a grubby portable dictionary.

The voice that came out of the polished brass speaker of the door entry system was a soft Spanish voice asking her, in French, to say who she was.

'My name is Isabel. Your visitor is waiting for you downstairs.'

A police siren drowned her out and she had to start again.

'Did you say your name is Isabel?' It was a simple enough question but it made her anxious, as if she was indeed pretending to be someone she was not.

The entry system made a whining sound and she pushed open the glass door framed in heavy dark wood that led into the marble foyer. The Russian woman in her stained dark glasses did not want to move and instead kept repeating her request to be taken to the port.

'Are you still there, Isabel?'

Why did the doctor not walk down the stairs and collect the blind woman himself?

'Could you come down and get your patient?' She heard him laugh.

'*Señora, soy doctor en filosofía.* She is not my patient. She is my student.'

He was laughing again. The dark rumbling laugh of a smoker. She heard his voice through the holes in the speaker and moved closer to it.

'My student wants the port because she wishes to go back to St Petersburg. She does not want to arrive for her Spanish lesson and therefore does not believe she is here. *Ella no quiere estar aquí.*'

He was playful and flirtatious, a man who had time to speak in riddles from the safety of the door entry system. She wished she could be more like him and fool around and play with whatever the day brought in. What had led her to where she was now? Where was she now? As usual she was running away from Jozef. This thought made her eyes sting with tears she resented. No, not again, not Jozef, not again. She turned away and left the Russian woman groping the banisters of the marble stairway, still insisting she was in the wrong place and the port was her final destination.

The sky had darkened and she could smell the sea somewhere close. Seagulls screeched above her head. The sweet yeasty smell of the *boulangerie* across the road wafted over the parked cars. Families were returning from the beach carrying plastic balls and chairs and colourful towels. The *boulangerie* was suddenly full of teenage boys buying slices of pizza. Across the road the mechanic was revving his motorbike triumphantly. She was not ready to go home and start imitating someone she used to be. Instead she walked for what seemed like an hour along the Promenade des Anglais and stopped at one of the restaurants set up on the beach near the airport.

The planes taking off flew low over the black sea. A party of students was drinking beer on the slopes of the pebbles. They were opinionated, flirtatious, shouting at each other, enjoying a summer night on the city beach. Things were starting in their lives. New jobs. New ideas. New friendships. New love affairs. She was in the middle of her life, she was nearly fifty years old and had witnessed countless massacres and conflicts in the work that pressed her up close to the suffering world. She had not been posted to cover the genocide in Rwanda, as two of her shattered colleagues had been. They had told her it was impossible to believe the scale of the human demolition, their own eyes dazed as they took in the dazed eyes of the orphans. Starved dogs had become accustomed to eating human flesh. They had seen dogs roam the fields with bits of people between their teeth. Yet even without witnessing first-hand the terrors of Rwanda, she had gone too far into the unhappiness of the world to start all over again. If she could choose to unlearn everything that was supposed to have made her wise, she would start all over again. Ignorant and hopeful, she would marry all over again and have a child all over again and drink beer with her handsome young husband on this city beach at night. They would be enchanted beginners all over again, kissing under the bright stars. That was the best thing to be in life.

A large extended family of women and their children sat at three tables pushed together. They all had the same wiry brown hair and high cheekbones and they were eating elaborate swirls of ice cream piled into pint-sized glasses. The waiter lit the sparklers he had stuck into the chantilly and they oohed and aahed and clapped their hands. She was cold in her halter-neck dress, too naked for this time of night. The women feeding their children with long silver teaspoons glanced curiously at the silent brooding woman with bare shoulders. Like the waiter, they seemed offended by her solitude. She had to tell him twice she was not expecting anyone to join her. When he slammed her espresso on the empty table set for two, most of it spilled into the saucer.

She watched the waves crash on the pebbles. The ocean folding into itself the plastic bags left on the beach that day. While she tried to make what was left of her coffee last long enough to earn her place at a table set for two, the thoughts she tried to push away kept returning like the waves on the stones.

She was a kind of ghost in her London home. When she returned to it from various war zones and found that in her absence the shoe polish or light bulbs had been put in a different place, somewhere similar but not quite where they were before, she learned that she too had a transient place in the family home. To do the things she had chosen to do in the world, she risked forfeiting her place as a wife and mother, a bewildering place haunted by all that had been imagined for her if she chose to sit in it. She had attempted to be someone she didn't really understand. A powerful but fragile female character. If she knew that to be forceful was not the same as being powerful and to be gentle was not the same as being fragile, she did not know how to use this knowledge in her own life or what it added up to, or even how it made sitting alone at a table laid for two on a Saturday night feel better. When she arrived in London from Africa or Ireland or Kuwait it was Laura who sometimes offered her a bed in the storeroom above their shop in Euston. It was a kind of convalescence. She lay on it in the daytime and Laura brought her cups of tea when the shop was quiet. They had nothing in common except they had known each other for a long time. The time that had passed between them counted for something. They did not have to explain anything or be polite or fill in the gaps in conversation.

She invited Laura to share the villa with them for the summer and was surprised at how quickly her friend accepted. Laura and Mitchell usually needed more notice to shut up the shop and get their affairs in order.

The sparklers were spluttering to an end in the ice creams. One of the mothers suddenly shouted at her five-year-old son, who had dropped his glass on the floor. It was a cry of incandescent rage. Isabel could see she was exhausted. The woman had become fierce, neither unhappy nor happy. She was now on her hands and knees, wiping the ice cream on the floor with the napkins the clan were holding out to her. She felt the disapproval of the women staring at her as she sat alone, but she was grateful to them. She would bring Nina to this restaurant and buy her daughter an ice cream with a sparkler in it. The women had planned something lovely for their children, something she would imitate.

Walls That Open and Close

Nina watched Kitty Finch press the palms of her hands against the walls of the spare bedroom as if she was testing how solid they were. It was a small room looking over the back of the villa, the yellow curtains drawn tight across the only window. It made the room hot and dark, but Kitty said she liked it that way. Upstairs in the kitchen they could hear Mitchell singing an Abba song out of tune. Kitty told Nina she was checking the walls because the foundations of the villa were shaky. Three years ago a gang of cowboy builders from Menton had been paid to patch the whole house together. There were cracks everywhere but they had been hastily covered up with the wrong sort of plaster.

Nina couldn't get over how much Kitty knew about everything. What was the right sort of plaster, then? Did Kitty Finch work in the construction industry? How did she manage to tuck all her hair into a hard hat?

It was as if Kitty had read her thoughts, because she said, 'Yeah, well, the right sort of plaster has limestone in it,' and then she knelt down on the floor and examined the plants she had collected in the churchyard earlier that morning.

Her green fingernails stroked the triangular leaves and clusters of white flowers that, she insisted, wrinkling her nose, smelt of mice. She was collecting the seeds from the plants because she wanted to study them and Nina could help her if she wanted to.

'What sort of plant is it?'

'It's called *Conium maculatum*. It comes from the same family as fennel, parsnips and carrot. I was really surprised to see it growing by the church. The leaves look like parsley, don't they?'

Nina didn't really know.

'This is hemlock. Your father knew that, of course. In the old days children used to make whistles from the stems and it sometimes poisoned them. But the Greeks thought it cured tumours.'

Kitty seemed to have a lot to do. After she'd hung up her summer dresses in the wardrobe and lined up a few tattered well-thumbed books on the shelf, she ran upstairs to look at the pool again, even though it was now dark outside.

When she came back she explained that the pool now had underwater lighting. 'It didn't last year.'

She took a brown A4 envelope out of the blue canvas bag and studied it. 'This,' she said, waving it at Nina, 'is the poem your father has promised to read tonight.' She chewed at her top lip. 'He said to put it on the table outside his bedroom. Will you come with me?'

Nina led Kitty Finch to the room where her parents slept. Their bedroom was the largest in the villa, with an even larger bathroom attached to it. It had gold taps and a power shower and a button to turn the bath into a jacuzzi. She pointed to a small table pushed against the wall outside their bedroom. A bowl stood in the centre of the table, a muddle of swimming goggles, dried flowers, old felt-tips, postcards and keys.

'Oh, those are the keys to the pump room.' Kitty sounded excited. 'The pump room stores all the machinery that makes the swimming pool work. I'll put the envelope under the bowl.'

She frowned at the brown envelope and kept taking deep breaths, shaking her curls as if something was caught in her hair.

'Actually, I think I'll slip it under the door. That way he'll trip over it and have to read it immediately.'

Nina was about to tell her that it wasn't his bedroom, her mother slept there too, but she stopped herself because Kitty Finch was saying weird things.

'You have to take a chance, don't you? It's like crossing a road with your eyes shut . . . you don't know what's going to happen next.' And then she threw back her head and laughed. 'Remind me to drive you to Nice tomorrow for the best ice cream you'll ever taste in your life.'

Standing next to Kitty Finch was like being near a cork that had just popped out of a bottle. The first pop when gasses seem to escape and everything is sprinkled for one second with something intoxicating.

Mitchell was calling them for supper.

Manners

'My wife is having her shoes mended in Nice,' Joe Jacobs announced theatrically to everyone at the dinner table.

His tone suggested he was merely giving information and required no reply from the audience assembled for dinner. They concurred. It was not mentioned.

Mitchell, always the self-appointed chef, had spent the afternoon roasting the hunk of beef Joe had insisted on paying for in the market that morning. He sliced it gleefully, pink blood oozing from its centre.

'None for me, thank you,' Kitty said politely.

'Oh, just a morsel.' A thin slice of bloody meat dropped from his fork and landed on her plate.

'Morsel is Mitchell's favourite word.' Joe picked up his napkin and tucked it into his shirt collar.

Laura poured the wine. She was wearing an ornate African necklace, a thick band of plaited gold fastened with seven pearls around her neck.

'You look like a bride,' Kitty said admiringly.

'Strangely enough,' Laura replied, 'this actually is a bridal necklace from our shop. It's from Kenya.'

Kitty's eyes were watering from the horseradish, which she spooned into her mouth as if it was sugar. 'So what do you and Mitchell sell at your "Cash and Carry"?'

'"Emporium",' Laura corrected her. 'We sell primitive Persian, Turkish and Hindu weapons. And expensive African jewellery.'

'We are small-time arms dealers,' Mitchell said effusive-ly. 'And in between we sell furniture made from ostriches.'

Joe rolled a slice of meat with his fingers and dipped it into the bowl of horseradish. 'Furniture is made from os-triches and horseradish is made from horses,' he chanted.

Nina flung down her knife. 'Shut the fuck up.'

Mitchell grimaced. 'Girls of your age shouldn't use such ugly words.'

Her father nodded as if he entirely agreed. Nina stared at him furiously as he polished his spoon with the end of the tablecloth. She knew her father had a lot of time for what Mitchell called 'ugly' words. When she told him, as she regu-larly did, that she was sick of wearing totally sad shoes to school with the wrong colour tights, her father the poet cor-rected her choice of words: 'Next time say totally sad *fucking* crap shoes. It will give your case more emphasis.'

'Ugly words are for ugly thoughts.' Mitchell briskly tapped the side of his bald head and then licked a smear of horseradish off his thumb. 'I never would have sworn in front of my father when I was your age.'

Joe shot his daughter a look. 'Yes, my child. Please don't swear like that and offend the fuckers at this table. Especial-ly Mitchell. He's dangerous. He's got weapons. Swords and ivory revolvers.'

'Ac-tu-ally' – Mitchell wagged his finger – 'what I really need is a mousetrap, because there are rodents in this kitchen.'

He glanced at Kitty Finch when he said 'rodents'.

Kitty dropped her slice of beef on the floor and leaned towards Nina. 'Horseradish is not made out of horses. It's related to the mustard family. It's a root and your father probably eats so much of it because it's good for his rheumatism.'

Joe raised his thick eyebrows. 'Whaat? I haven't got rheumatism!'

'You probably have,' Kitty replied. 'You're a bit stiff when you walk.'

'That's because he's old enough to be your father,' Laura smiled nastily. She was still puzzled why Isabel had been so insistent that a young woman, who swam naked and obviously wanted her middle-aged husband's attention should stay with them. Her friend was supposed to be the betrayed partner in their marriage. Hurt by his infidelities. Burdened by his past. Betrayed and lied to.

'Laura congratulates herself on seeing through people and talking straight,' Joe declared to the table. He squeezed the tip of his nose between his finger and thumb, a secret code between himself and his daughter, of what he wasn't sure, perhaps of enduring love despite his flaws and foolishness and their mutual irritations with each other.

Kitty smiled nervously at Laura. 'Thank you all so much for letting me stay.'

Nina watched her nibble on a slice of cucumber and then push it to the side of her plate.

'You should thank Isabel,' Laura corrected her. 'She is very kind-hearted.'

'I wouldn't say Isabel is kind, would you, Nina?'

Joe rolled another slice of bloody beef and pushed it into his mouth.

This was the cue for Nina to say something critical

about her mother to please her father, something like, 'My mother doesn't know me at all.' In fact she was tempted to say, 'My mother doesn't know I know my father will sleep with Kitty Finch. She doesn't even know I know what anorexic means.'

Instead she said, 'Kitty thinks walls can open and close.'

When Mitchell whirled his left forefinger in circles around his ear as if to say, crazeee she's crazeee, Joe reached over and violently slapped down Mitchell's teasing pink finger with his tight brown fist.

'It's rude to be so normal, Mitchell. Even you must have been a child once. Even you might have thought there were monsters lurking under your bed. Now that you are such an impeccably normal adult you probably take a discreet look under the bed and tell yourself, well, maybe the monster is invisible!'

Mitchell rolled his eyes and stared at the ceiling as if pleading with it for help and advice. 'Has anyone ever actually told you how up yourself you are?

The telephone was ringing. A fax was sliding and grinding its way on to the plastic tray next to the villa's fact file. Nina stood up and walked over to pick it up. She glanced at it and brought it to her father.

'It's for you. About your reading in Poland.'

'Thank you.' He kissed her hand with his wine-stained lips and told her to read the fax out loud to him.

LUNCH ON ARRIVAL.
TWO MENUS. White borscht with boiled egg and sausage.
Traditional hunter's stew with mash potatoes. Soft drink.
OR
Traditional Polish cucumber soup. Cabbage leaves stuffed
with meat and mash potatoes. Soft drink.
KINDLY FAX YOUR CHOICE.

Laura coughed. 'You were born in Poland, weren't you, Joe?'

Nina watched her father shake his head vaguely.

'I don't remember.'

Mitchell raised his eyebrows in what he imagined was disbelief. 'You got to be a bit forgetful not to remember where you were born. You're Jewish, aren't you, sir?'

Joe looked startled. Nina wondered if it was because her father had been called sir. Kitty was frowning too. She sat up straighter in her chair and addressed the table as if she was Joe's biographer.

'Of course he was born in Poland. It's on all his book jackets. Jozef Nowogrodzki was born in western Poland in 1937. He arrived in Whitechapel, east London, when he was five years old.'

'Right.' Mitchell looked confused again. 'So how come you're Joe Jacobs, then?'

Kitty once again took charge. She might as well have pinged her wine glass three times to create an expectant silence. 'The teachers at his boarding school changed his name so they could spell it.'

The spoon Joe had been polishing all through supper was now silver and shiny. When he held it up as if to inspect his hard work, Nina could see Kitty's distorted reflection floating on the back of it.

'Boarding school? Where were your parents, then?'

Mitchell noticed that Laura was squirming in her chair. Whatever it was he was supposed to know about Joe had totally gone from his mind. Laura had told him of course, but it hadn't sunk in. He was relieved Kitty Finch did not take it upon herself to answer his question and sort of wished he hadn't gone there.

'Well, you're more or less English, then, aren't you, Joe?'

Joe nodded. 'Yes, I am. I'm nearly as English as you are.'

'Well, I wouldn't go along all the way with that, Joe,' Mitchell asserted in the tone of a convivial customs official, 'but, as I always say to Laura, it's what we feel inside that counts.'

'You're right,' Joe agreed.

Mitchell thought he was on to something because Joe was being polite for a change.

'So what do you feel inside, Joe?'

Joe peered at the spoon in his hand as if it was a jewel or a small triumph over cloudy cutlery.

'I've got an FFF inside.'

'What's that, sir?'

'A fucking funny feeling.'

Mitchell, who was now drunk, slapped him on the back to confirm their new solidarity.

'I'll second that, Jozef whatever your surname is. I've

got an FFF right here.' He tapped his head. 'I've got three of those.'

Laura shuffled her long feet under the table and announced she had made a trifle for pudding. It was a recipe she had taken from Delia Smith's *Complete Cookery Course* and she hoped the custard had set and the cream hadn't curdled.

SUNDAY

Hemlock Thief

The beginning of birdsong. The sound of pine cones falling into the stillness of the pool. The harsh scent of rosemary growing in wooden crates on the window ledge. When Kitty Finch woke up she felt someone breathing on her face. At first she thought the window had blown open in the night, but then she saw him and had to shove her hair into her mouth to stop herself screaming out loud. A black-haired boy was standing by her bed and he was waving to her. She guessed he was fifteen years old and he was holding a notebook in the hand that was not waving. The notebook was yellow. He was wearing a school blazer and his tie was stuffed in his pocket. Eventually he disappeared into the wall, but she could still feel the breeze of his invisible waving hand.

He was inside her. He had trance-journeyed into her mind. She was receiving his thoughts and feelings and his intentions. She dug her fingernails into her cheeks and, when she was sure she was awake, she walked towards the French doors and climbed into the pool. A wasp stung her wrist as she swam to the half-deflated lilo and pulled it to the shallow end. She wasn't sure if the spectral vision was a ghost or a dream or a hallucination. Whatever it was, he had been in her mind for a long time. She plunged her head under the water and started to count to ten.

Someone was in the pool with her.

Kitty could just make out the magnified tips of Isabel Jacobs' fingers scooping up insects that were always dying in the deep end. When she surfaced, Isabel's strong arms were now slicing through the cold green water, the insects writhing in a pile on the paving stone nearest the pool's edge. The journalist wife, so silent and superior, apparently disappeared to Nice at mealtimes and no one talked about it. Least of all her husband, who, Kitty hoped, had read her poem by now. That's what he said he was going to do after the endless supper last night. He was going to lie on his bed and read her words.

'You're shivering, Kitty.'

Isabel swam towards her until the two women stood shoulder-to-shoulder, watching the early-morning mist rise from the mountains. She told Isabel she had earache and she was feeling dizzy. It was the only way she could talk about what she had seen that morning.

'You probably have an ear infection. It's not surprising you're unsteady on your feet.'

Isabel was trying to sound like she was in control of everything. Kitty had seen her on the television about three years ago. Isabel Jacobs standing in the desert near a camel skeleton in Kuwait. She was leaning on a burnt-out army tank, pointing to a charred pair of soldier's boots lying underneath it. Elegant and groomed, Isabel Jacobs was meaner than she looked. When she had dived into the pool yesterday and grabbed Kitty's ankle, she had twisted it hard enough to give her a Chinese burn. Her foot still hurt from that. Isabel had hurt her deliberately, but Kitty couldn't say anything because the next thing she did was offer her the spare room. No one dared say they minded, because the war correspondent was controlling them all. Like she had the final word or was daring them to contradict her. The truth was her husband had the final word because he wrote words and then he put full stops at the end of them. She knew this, but what did his wife know?

Kitty leapt out of the water and walked to the edge of the pool, picking bay leaves off a small tree that grew in a pot by the shallow end. Isabel got out too and sat on the edge of a white recliner. The journalist wife was lighting a cigarette absent-mindedly, as if she was thinking about something more important than what was happening now. She must have seen the battered A4 envelope Kitty had left propped against the bedroom door.

Swimming Home

by

Kitty Finch

She did not tell Isabel that she was feeling hot and her vision was blurred. Her skin was itching and she thought her tongue might be swollen too. Nor did she tell her about the spectral boy who had walked out of the wall to greet her when she woke up. He had stolen some of her plants, because when he walked back into the wall he had a bundle of them in his arms. She thought he might be searching for ways to die. The words she heard him say were words she heard in her head and not with her ears. He was waving as if to greet her, but now she thought he might have been saying goodbye.

'So did you come here because you're a fan of Jozef's poetry?'

Kitty chewed slowly on a silver bay leaf until she could mask the anxiety in her voice. 'I suppose I am a fan. Though I don't see it like that.'

She paused, waiting for her voice to steady itself. 'Joe's poetry is more like a conversation with me than anything else. He writes about things I often think. We are in nerve contact.'

She turned round to see Isabel stub out her cigarette with her bare foot. Kitty gasped.

'Didn't that hurt?'

If Isabel had burned herself she seemed not to care.

'What does "nerve contact" with Jozef mean?'

'It doesn't mean anything. I just thought of it now.'

Kitty noticed how Isabel Jacobs always used her husband's full name. As if she alone owned the part of him that was secret and mysterious, the part of him that wrote things. How could she tell her that she and Joe were transmitting messages to each other when she didn't understand it herself? This was something she would discuss with Jurgen. He would explain that she had extra senses because she was a poet and then he would say words to her in German that she knew were love words. It was always tricky to get away from him at night, so she was grateful to have the spare room to escape to. Yes, in a way she was grateful to Isabel for saving her from Jurgen's love.

'What's your poem about?'

Kitty studied the bay leaf, her fingertips tracing the outline of its silver veins.

'I can't remember.'

Isabel laughed. This was offensive. Kitty was offended. No longer grateful, she glared at the woman who had offered her the spare room but had not bothered to provide sheets or pillows or notice the windows did not open and the floor was covered in mouse droppings. The journalist was asking her questions as if she was about to file her copy. She was curvaceous and tall, her black hair dark as an Indian woman's, and she wore a gold band on her left hand to show she was married. Her fingers were long and smooth, like she'd never scrubbed a pot clean or poked her fingers into the earth. She had not even bothered to offer her guest a few clothes hangers. Nina had had to bring down an armful from her own cupboard. Nevertheless Isabel Jacobs was still asking questions, because she wanted to be in control.

'You said you know the owner of this villa?'

'Yeah. She's a shrink called Rita Dwighter and she's a friend of my mother's. She's got houses everywhere. In fact she's got twelve properties in London alone worth about two million each. She probably asks her patients if they've got a mortgage.'

Isabel laughed and this time Kitty laughed too.

'Thank you for letting me stay, by the way.'

Isabel nodded dismissively and said something about going inside to make toast and honey. Kitty watched her run through the glass doors, bumping into Laura, who was now sitting at the kitchen table, a pair of earphones clamped on her head and a tangle of wires around her neck. Laura was learning some sort of African language, her thin lips mouthing the words out loud.

Kitty sat naked and shivering at the end of the pool, listening to the tall blonde woman with scared blue eyes repeat singsong sentences from another continent. She could hear the church bells ringing in the village and she could hear someone sighing. When she looked up she had to stop herself from losing it for the second time that morning. Madeleine Sheridan was sitting on her balcony as usual, staring at her as if she was scanning the ocean for a shark. That was too much. Kitty jumped up and shook her fist at the shadowy figure drinking her morning tea.

'Don't fucking watch me all the time. I'm still waiting for you to get my shoes, Dr Sheridan. Have you got them yet?'

Homesick Aliens

Jurgen was dragging an inflatable three-foot rubber alien with a wrinkled neck into the kitchen of Claude's café. He had bought it at the flea market on Saturday and he and Claude were having three conversations at once. Claude, who had only just turned twenty-three and knew he looked like Mick Jagger, owned the only café in the village and was planning to sell it to Parisian property developers next year. What Claude wanted to know was why the tourists had offered Kitty Finch a room.

Jurgen scratched his scalp and swung his dreadlocks to get an angle on the question. The effort was exhausting him and he could not find an answer. Claude, whose silky shoulder-length hair was expensively cut to make it look as if he never bothered with it, reckoned Kitty must secretly be repulsed by the dreadlocks Jurgen cultivated, because she knew she could stay with him whenever she wanted. At the same time they were both jeering at Mitchell, who was sitting on the terrace stuffing himself with baguettes and jam while he waited for the grocery store to open. The fat man with his collection of old guns was running up a tab at the café *and* the grocery store, which was run by Claude's mother. Mitchell was going to bankrupt Claude's entire family. Meanwhile Jurgen was explaining the plot of the film *ET* while Claude peeled potatoes. Jurgen whipped the cigarette butt out of his friend's thick lips and sucked on it while he tried to remember the film he'd seen in Monaco three years ago.

'ET is this baby alien who finds himself lost on earth,

three million light years away from home. He makes friends with a ten-year-old boy and they start to have a very special connection with each other.'

Claude gave the little alien in his kitchen a leering wink. 'What sort of connection?'

Jurgen swung his dreadlocks over a freshly baked pear tart cooling under the kitchen window as if to summon a plot he had long forgotten.

'So . . . if ET gets sick the earth boy gets sick, if ET is hungry earth boy gets hungry, if ET is tired or sad then earth boy suffers with him. The alien and his friend are in touch with each other's thoughts. They are mentally connected.'

Claude grimaced, because he was being called by Mitchell for another basket of bread and a slice of the pear tart, newly written into the menu. Claude told Jurgen he couldn't work out why the fat man never had any money on him despite staying in the luxurious villa. His tab had gone off the scale. 'So anyway how does *ET* end?'

Jurgen, who was usually too stoned to remember anything, had just spotted Joe Jacobs in the distance, walking among the sheep grazing in the mountains. For some reason he could remember every line the baby alien uttered in the film. He thought this was because he was also an alien, a German nature boy living in France. He explained that ET has to disconnect himself from the boy because he fears he will make him too sick and he doesn't want to harm him. And then he finds a way of getting home to his own planet.

Jurgen nudged Claude and pointed to the English poet in the distance. He looked like he was saluting something invisible, because his fingers were touching his forehead. Claude quite liked the poet, because he always left big tips and had somehow managed to produce a gorgeous, long-legged teenage daughter whom Claude had personally invited to the café for an aperitif. So far she had not taken him up on his offer, but he lived in hope because, as he told Jurgen, what else was there to live in?

'He is superstitious, he's just seen a magpie. He is famous. Do you want to be famous?'

Jurgen nodded. And then shook his head and helped himself to a swig from a bottle of green liquid leaning against the cooking oil.

'Yes. Sometimes I think it would be nice to no longer be a caretaker and everyone wants to kiss my arse. But there is one problem. I don't have the energy to be famous. I have too much to do.'

Claude pointed to the poet, who looked like he was still saluting magpies.

'Perhaps he is homesick. He wants to go home to his planet.'

Jurgen gargled with the green drink that Claude knew was mint syrup. Jurgen was more or less addicted to it in the same way some people are addicted to absinthe, which had the same fairy green colour.

'No. He is just avoiding Kitty Ket. He has not read Ket's thing and he is avoiding her. The Ket is like ET. She thinks she has a mental connection with the poet. He has not read her thing and she will be sad and her blood pressure will go up and she will murder them all with the fat man's guns.'

MONDAY

The Trapper

Mitchell lay on his back sweating. It was three a.m. and he had just had a nightmare about a centipede. He had hacked it with a carving knife but it split in two and started to grow again. The more he hacked at it the more centipedes there were. They writhed at his feet. He was up to his ears in centipedes and the blade of his knife was covered in slime. They were crawling into his nostrils and trying to get into his mouth. When he woke up he wondered if he should tell Laura his heart was pounding so hard and fast he thought he might be about to have a heart attack. Laura was sleeping peacefully on her side, her feet poking out of the bed. There was no bed in the world that was long enough for Laura. Their bed in London had been specially designed for her height and his width by a Danish shipbuilder. It took up the whole room and resembled a galleon beached on a pond in a civic park. Something was crawling towards him along the whitewashed wall. He screamed.

'What is it, Mitch?' Laura sat up and put her hand on her husband's heaving chest.

He pointed to the thing on the wall.

'It's a moth, Mitchell.'

Sure enough it spread its grey wings and flew out of the window.

'I had a nightmare,' he grunted. 'A terrible, terrible nightmare.'

She squeezed his hot clammy hand. 'Go back to sleep. You'll feel better in the morning.' She tugged the sheet over her shoulder and lay down again.

There was no way he could sleep. Mitchell got up and walked upstairs to the kitchen, where he felt most safe. He opened the fridge and reached for a bottle of water. As he put the bottle to his lips and thirstily gulped down the iced water, he felt in bits and pieces like the centipede. When he lifted up his aching head, he noticed something lying on the kitchen floor. It was the trap he had set for the rat. He had caught something. He swallowed hard and made his way towards it.

A small animal was lying on its side with its back to him, but it was not a rat. He recognised the creature. It was Nina's brown nylon rabbit, its long floppy ear stapled under the wire. He could see its worn white ball of a tail and the grubby label sewn inside its leg. The green satin ribbon around its neck had somehow got tangled in the wires too. He found himself sweating as he bent down to free it from the wire and then noticed a shadow on the floor. Someone was there with him. Someone had broken into the villa and he didn't have his guns with him. Even his ancient ebony weapon from Persia would see off whoever was there.

'Hello, Mitchell.'

Kitty Finch was leaning naked against the wall, watching him struggle not to catch his fingers in his own trap. She was nibbling the chocolate he had left for the rat, her arms folded across her breasts.

'I call you the trapper now, but I've warned all the owls about you.'

He pressed his hand on his pounding heart and stared at her pale, righteous face. He would shoot her. If he had his weapons with him he would do it. He would aim for her stomach. He imagined how he would hold the gun and timed the moment he would snap the trigger. She would fall to the ground, her glassy grey eyes wide open, a bloody hole gouged in her belly. He blinked and saw she was still standing against the wall, taunting him with the chocolate he had placed so carefully in the wires. She looked thin and pathetic and he realised he had scared her.

'Sorry I was so abrupt.'

'Yeah.' She nodded as if they were suddenly best friends. 'You gave me a fright, but I was frightened anyway.'

He was terrified too. For a moment he seriously considered telling her about his nightmare.

'Why do you kill animals and birds, Mitchell?'

She was almost pretty, with her narrow waist and long hair glowing in the dark, but ragged too, not far off someone begging outside a train station holding up a homeless and hungry sign.

'It takes my mind off things,' he found himself saying as if he meant it, which he did.

'What sorts of things?'

Again he considered telling her about some of the worries that weighed heavily on his mind but stopped himself just in time. He couldn't go shooting his mouth off to someone crazy like her.

'You're a complete fuck-up, Mitchell. Stop killing things and you'll feel better.'

'Haven't you got a home to go to?' He thought he had meant this quite kindly, but even to his own ears it sounded like an insult.

'Yeah, I live with my mother at the moment, but it's not my home.'

As she knelt down to help him untangle the grubby toy rabbit that made a mockery of his trap, he couldn't work out why he thought someone as sad as she was might be dangerous.

'You know what?' This time Mitchell thought he genuinely meant this kindly. 'If you wore clothes more often instead of walking around in your birthday suit, you'd look more normal.'

Spirited Away

Nina's disappearance was only discovered at seven a.m. after Joe called for her because he had lost his special ink pen. His daughter was the person who always found it for him, whatever the time, a drama Laura had heard at least twelve times that holiday. Whenever Nina returned the pen victoriously to her loud, forlorn father he wrapped her in his arms and bellowed melodramatically, 'Thank you thank you thank you.' Often in a number of languages: Polish, Portuguese, Italian. Yesterday it was, *'Danke danke danke.'*

No one could believe Joe was actually shouting for his daughter to find his pen so early in the morning, but that was what he did and Nina did not answer. Isabel walked into her daughter's bedroom and saw the doors to her balcony were wide open. She whipped off the duvet, expecting to see her hiding under the covers. Nina wasn't there and the sheet was stained with blood. When Laura heard Isabel sobbing, she ran into the room to find her friend pointing to the bed, strange choking sounds coming out of her mouth. She was pale, deathly white, uttering words that sounded to Laura like 'bone' or 'hair' or 'she isn't there'; it was hard to make sense of what she was saying.

Laura suggested they go together to look for Nina in the garden and steered her out of the room. Small birds swooped down to drink from the still, green water of the pool. A box of cherry chocolates from the day before lay melting on Mitchell's big blue chair, covered in ants. Two damp towels were draped on the canvas recliners and in the middle of them, like an interrupted conversation, was the wooden chair Isabel had dragged out for Kitty Finch. Under it was Joe's black ink pen.

This was the rearranged space of yesterday. They walked through the cypress trees and into the parched garden. It had not rained for months and Jurgen had forgotten to water the plants. The honeysuckle was dying, the soil beneath the brown grass cracked and hard. Under the tallest pine tree, Laura saw Nina's wet bikini lying on the pine needles. When she bent down to pick it up, even she could not help thinking the cherry print on the material looked like splashes of blood. Her fingers started to fumble in her pocket for the little stainless-steel calculator she and Mitchell had brought with them to do their accounts.

'Nina's OK, Isabel.' She ran her fingers over the calculator as if the numbers and symbols she knew were there, the m+ and m−, the x and the decimal point, would somehow end in Nina's appearance. 'She's probably gone for a walk. I mean, she's fourteen you know, she really has not been' – she was about to say 'slaughtered' but changed her mind and said 'spirited away' instead.

She didn't finish her sentence because Isabel was running through the cypress trees so fast and with such force the trees were shaking for minutes afterwards. Laura watched the momentary chaos of the trees. It was as if they had been pushed off balance and did not quite know how to find their former shape.

Mothers and Daughters

The spare room was dark and hot because the windows were closed and the curtains drawn. A pair of grubby flip-flops lay on top of the tangle of drying weeds lying on the floor. Kitty's red hair streamed over a lumpy stained pillow, her freckled arms wrapped around Nina, who was clutching the nylon fur rabbit that was her last embarrassed link with childhood. Isabel knew Nina was awake and that she was pretending to be asleep under what seemed to be a starched white tablecloth. It looked like a shroud.

'Nina, get up.' Isabel's voice was sharper than she meant it to be.

Kitty opened her grey eyes and whispered, 'Nina started her period in the night so she got into bed with me.'

The girls were drowsy and content in each other's arms. Isabel noticed the tattered books Kitty had put on the shelves, about six of them, were all her husband's books. Two pink rosebuds stood in a glass of water next to them. Roses that could only have been picked from Madeleine Sheridan's front garden, her attempt to create a memory of England in France.

She remembered Kitty's strange comment yesterday morning, after their swim together: 'Joe's poetry is a more like a conversation with me than anything else.' What sort of conversation was Kitty Finch having with her husband? Should she insist her daughter get out of bed and leave this room that was as hot as a greenhouse? Kitty was obviously trapping energy to heat her plants. She had made a small, hot, chaotic world, full of books and fruit and flowers, a substate in the country of the tourist villa with its Matisse and Picasso prints clumsily framed and hanging on the walls. Two plump bumblebees crawled down the yellow curtains, searching for an open window. The cupboard was open and Isabel glimpsed a short white feather cape hanging in the corner. Slim and pretty in her flip-flops and ragged summer dresses, it would seem Kitty Finch could make herself at home anywhere. Should she insist that Nina get up and return to her clean lonely room upstairs? Tearing her away from Kitty's arms felt like a violent thing to do. She bent down and kissed her daughter's dark eyebrow, which was twitching slightly.

'Come and say hello when you're awake.'

Nina's eyes were shut extra tight. Isabel closed the door.

When she walked into the kitchen she told Jozef and Laura that Nina was sleeping with Kitty.

'Ah. Thought as much.' Her husband scratched the back of his neck and disappeared into the garden to get his pen, which, Laura informed him, was 'under Kitty's chair'. He had covered his bare shoulders with a white pillowcase and looked like a self-ordained holy man. He did this to stop his shoulders burning when he wrote in the sun, but it infuriated Laura all the same. When she looked at him again he was examining the gold nib as if it had been damaged in some way. She opened the fridge. Mitchell wanted a piece of stale cheese to trap the brown rat he had seen scuttling about in the kitchen at night. It had gnawed through the salami hung on a hook above the sink and he'd had to throw it away. Mitchell was not so much squeamish as outraged by the vermin who devoured the morsels he bought with his hard-earned money. He took it personally, as if slowly but surely the rats were gnawing through his wallet.

Fathers and Daughters

So his lost daughter was asleep in Kitty's bed. Joe sat in the garden at his makeshift desk, waiting for the panic that had made his fingers tear the back of his neck to calm as he watched his wife talking to Laura inside the villa. His breathing was all over the place, he was fighting to breathe. Did he think Kitty Finch, who had stopped taking Seroxat and must be suffering, had lost her grip and murdered his daughter? His wife was now walking towards him through the gaps in the cypress trees. He shifted his legs as if part of him wanted to run away from her or perhaps run towards her. He truly did not know which way to go. He could try to tell Isabel something, but he wasn't sure how to begin because he wasn't sure how it would end. There were times he thought she could barely look at him without hiding her face in her hair. And he could not look at her either, because he had betrayed her so often. Perhaps now he should at least try and tell her that when she abandoned her young daughter to lie in a tent crawling with scorpions, he understood it made more sense of her life to be shot at in war zones than lied to by him in the safety of her own home. All the same, he knew his daughter had cried for her in the early years, and then later learned not to because it didn't bring her back. In turn (this subject turned and turned and turned regularly in his mind), his daughter's distress brought to him, her father, feelings he could not handle with dignity. He had told his readers how he was sent to boarding school by his guardians and how he used to watch the parents of his school friends leave on visiting day (Sundays), and if his own parents had visited him too, he would have stood for ever in the tyre marks their car had made in the dust. His mother and father were night visitors, not afternoon visitors. They appeared to him in dreams he instantly forgot, but he reckoned they were trying to find him. What had worried him most was he thought they might not have enough English words between them to make themselves understood. Is Jozef my son here? We have been looking for him all over the world. He had cried for them and then later learned not to because it didn't bring them back. He looked at his clever tanned wife with her dark hair hiding her face. This was the conversation that might start something or end something, but it came out wrong, just too random and fucked. He heard himself ask her if she liked honey.

'Yes. Why?'

'Because I know so little about you, Isabel.'

He would poke his paw inside every hollow of every tree to scoop up the honeycomb and lay it at her feet if he thought she might stay a little longer with him and their cub. She looked hostile and lonely and he understood it. He obviously disgusted her. She even preferred Mitchell's company to his.

He heard her say, 'The main thing to do for the rest of the summer is to make sure Nina is all right.'

'Of course Nina is all right,' he snapped. 'I've looked after her since she was three years old and she's bloody all right, isn't she?'

And then he took out his notebook and the black ink

pen that had disappeared that morning, knowing that Isabel was defeated every time he appeared to be writing and every time he talked about their daughter. These were his weapons to silence his wife and keep her in his life, to keep his family intact, flawed and hostile but still a family. His daughter was his main triumph in their marriage, the one thing he had done right.

– *yes yes yes she said yes yes yes she likes honey* – his pen scratched these words aggressively across the page while he watched a white butterfly hover above the pool. It was like breath. It was a miracle. A wonder. He and his wife knew things it was impossible to know. They had both seen life snuffed out. Isabel recorded and witnessed catastrophes to try and make people remember. He tried to make himself forget.

Collecting Stones

'It has a hole in the middle.'

Kitty held up a pebble the size of her hand and gave it to Nina to look through. They were sitting on one of the public beaches in Nice below the Promenade des Anglais. Kitty said on the private beaches they had to pay a fortune for sun-loungers and umbrellas. Everyone looked like patients on hospital beds and gave her the creeps. The sun was burning pink blotches in her waxy pale face.

Nina obediently looked through the hole. She saw a young woman smiling, a purple jewel drilled into her front tooth. When she turned the pebble round the woman was unpacking a carrier bag of food. There was another woman there too, sitting on a low striped canvas chair, and she was holding a large white dog by the lead with her right hand. The dog looked like a snow wolf. A husky with blue eyes. Nina stared into its blue eyes from the hole in the pebble. She couldn't be sure of this but she thought the snow wolf was undoing the shoelaces of the woman with the jewel in her tooth. Nina saw all of this in fragments through the hole in the pebble. When she looked again she saw the woman in the black T-shirt only had one arm. She turned the pebble lengthways and peered through it, squeezing her eye half shut. An electric wheelchair decorated with shells was parked near the canvas chair. Now the women were kissing. Like lovers. Watching them lean into each other, Nina heard her own breath get louder. She had been thinking all holiday about what she would do if she ever found herself alone with Claude. He had invited her to come to his café for what he described as an aperitif. She wasn't sure what that was and anyway something had happened that changed everything.

Last night when she woke up she discovered she was menstruating for the first time. She had dared herself to put on her bikini because it was the only thing she could find and knock on Kitty's door to tell her the news. Kitty was lying awake under an old tablecloth and she had rolled up one of her dresses to make a pillow.

'I've started.'

At first Kitty didn't know what she meant. And then she grabbed Nina's hand and they ran into the garden. Nina could see her own shadow in the pool and in the sky at the same time. She was tall and long, there was no end to her and no beginning, her body stretched out and vast. She wanted to swim and when Kitty insisted it didn't matter about the blood, she dared herself to take off her bikini and be naked, watching her twin shadow untie the straps more bravely than the real-sized Nina actually felt. She finally jumped into the pool and hid herself in the blanket of leaves that floated in the water, not sure what to do with her new body because it was morphing into something alien and perplexing to her.

Kitty swam over and pointed to the silver snails on the paving stones. She said the stars laid their dust over everything. There were bits of broken stars on the snails. And then she blinked.

blah blah blah blah blah blinked

Standing naked in the water, Nina pretended she had a serious speech impediment and made stammering sounds in her head. She felt like someone else. Like someone who had started. Someone who wasn't her. She felt unbearably happy and plunged her head into the water to celebrate the miracle of Kitty Finch's arrival. She was not alone with Laura and Mitchell and her mother and father who she wasn't sure liked each other never mind loved each other.

Nina threw the pebble into the sea, which seemed to annoy Kitty. She stood up and yanked Nina up too.

'I need to collect more pebbles. That one you threw away was perfect.'

'Why do you want them?'

'To study them.'

Nina was hobbling because her trainers were rubbing up against the blisters on the back of her heels. 'They're too heavy to carry,' she groaned. 'I want to go now.'

Kitty was sweating and her breath smelt sweet.

'Yeah, well, sorry to waste your time. Have you ever cleaned a floor, Nina? Ever got down on your hands and knees with a rag while your mother screams at you to clean the corners? Have you ever hoovered the stairs and taken out the bin bags?'

The pampered girl in her pricey shorts (she had seen the label) and all her split ends trimmed had obviously got to fourteen years old without lifting a finger.

'You need some real problems to take back to your posh house in London with you.'

She flung down the rucksack full of pebbles and marched into the sea in the butter-coloured dress she said made her feel extra cheerful. Nina watched her dive into a wave. The house in London Kitty referred to wasn't exactly cosy. Her father always in his study. Her mother away, her shoes and dresses lined up in the wardrobe like someone who had died. When she was seven and always had nits in her hair the house had smelt of the magic potions she used to make from her mother's face creams and her father's shaving foam. The big house in west London smelt of other things too. Of her father's girlfriends and their various shampoos. And of her father's perfume, made for him by a Swiss woman from Zurich who married a man who owned two show horses in Bulgaria. He said her perfumes 'opened his mind', especially his favourite, which was called Hungary Water. The posh house smelt of his special status and of the sheets he always put in the washing machine after his girlfriends left in the morning. And of the apricot jam he spooned into his mouth straight from the jar. He said the jam changed the weather inside him, but she didn't know what the weather was in the first place.

She did sort of know. Sometimes when she walked into his study she thought he looked a sorry sight stooped in his dressing gown, silent and still as if he'd been pinned down by something. She'd got used to the days he was sunk in his chair and refused to look at her or even get up for nights on end. She'd close the door of his study and bring him mugs of tea he never touched, because they were still there when she talked to him from behind the door (a slimy beige skin grown over the tea) and asked him for lunch money or to sign a letter giving his permission for a school trip. In the end she signed them herself with his ink pen, which is why she always knew where it was, usually under her bed or upside down in the bathroom with the toothbrushes. She had designed a signature she could always replicate, J.H.J with a full stop between the letters and a flourish on the last J. After a while he usually cheered up and took her to the Angus Steak House, where they sat on the same faded red velvet banquette they always sat on. They never talked about his own childhood or his girlfriends. This was not so much an unspoken secret pact between them, more like having a tiny splinter of glass in the sole of her foot, always there, slightly painful, but she could live with it.

When Kitty came back, her dress dripping wet, she was saying something but the husky was barking at a seagull. Nina could just see Kitty's lips moving and she knew, with an aching feeling inside her, that she was still angry or something was wrong. As they walked to the car Kitty said, 'I'm meeting your father at Claude's café tomorrow. He's going to talk to me about my poem. Nina, I am so nervous. I should have got a summer job in a pub in London and not bothered. I don't know what's going to happen.'

Nina wasn't listening. She had just seen a boy in silver shorts roller-skating down the esplanade with a bag of lemons tucked under his tanned arm. He looked a bit like Claude but he wasn't. When she heard a bird screeching in what she thought sounded like agony, she dared not look back at the beach. She thought the husky or snow wolf might have caught the seagull after all. Maybe it wasn't happening and anyway she had just spotted the old lady who lived next door walking on the promenade. She was talking to Jurgen, who was wearing purple sunglasses in the shape of hearts. Nina called out and waved.

'That's Madeleine Sheridan, our neighbour.'

Kitty gazed up. 'Yes, I know. The evil old witch.'

'Is she?'

'Yes. She calls me Katherine and she nearly killed me.'

After she said that, Kitty did something so spooky that Nina told herself she hadn't seen it properly. She leaned backwards so that her copper hair rippled down the back of her knees and shook her head from side to side very fast while her hands jerked and flailed above her head. Nina could see the fillings in her teeth. And then she lifted her head up and gave Madeleine Sheridan the finger.

Kitty Finch was mental.

Medical Help from Odessa

Madeleine Sheridan was trying to pay for a scoop of caramel-ised nuts she had bought from the Mexican vendor on the esplanade. The smell of burnt sugar made her greedy for the nuts that would at last, she hoped, choke her to death. Her nails were crumbling, her bones weakening, her hair thinning, her waist gone for ever. She had turned into a toad in old age and if anyone dared to kiss her she would not turn back into a princess because she had never been a princess in the first place.

'These damn coins. What's this one, Jurgen?' Before Jurgen could answer she whispered, 'Did you see Kitty Finch doing *that thing* to me?'

He shrugged. 'Sure. Kitty Ket has something to say to you. But now she has some new friends to make her happy. I have to book the horse-riding for Nina. The Ket will take her.'

She let him take her arm and steer her (a little too fast) into one of the bars on the beach. He was the only person she talked to in any detail about her life in England and her es-cape from her marriage. She appreciated his stupor, it made him non-judgemental. Despite the difference in their age she enjoyed his company. Having nothing to do in life but live off other people and his wits, he always made her feel dignified rather than a sad case, probably because he wasn't listening.

Today she was barely listening to him. The arrival of Kitty Finch was bad news. This is what she was thinking as she stared at a motorboat making white frothy scars on the chalky-blue sea. When he found a table in the shade and helped her into a chair that was much too small for a toad, he seemed not to realise she would have to twist her body into positions that made her ache. It was thoughtless of him, but she was too disorientated by the sight of Kitty Finch to care.

She tried to calm herself by insisting Jurgen take off his sunglasses.

'It's like looking into two black holes, Jurgen.'

It was her birthday in four days' time and right now she was thirsty in the heat, almost crazed with thirst. She had been looking forward to their lunch appointment for weeks. That morning she had telephoned her favourite restaurant to find out what was on the menu, where their table was positioned and to request the maître d' save her a parking space right outside the door in return for a healthy tip. She screamed at a waiter for a whisky and a Pepsi for Jurgen, who disliked alcohol for spiritual reasons. It was hard for an old woman to get a waiter's attention when he was busy serving topless women sunbathing in thongs. She had read about yogic *siddhas* who mastered human invisibility through a combination of concentration and meditation. Somehow she had managed to make her body imperceptible to the waiter without any of the training. She lifted both her arms and waved at him as if she were flagging down an aeroplane on a desert island. Jurgen pointed to the accordion player from Marseilles perched on a wooden box by the flashing pinball machine. The musician was sweating in a black suit three sizes too large for him.

'He's playing at a wedding this afternoon. The beekeeper from Valbonne told me. If I got married I would ask him to play at my wedding too.'

Madeleine Sheridan, sipping her hard-won whisky, was surprised at how his voice was suddenly so high-pitched.

'Marriage is not a good idea, Jurgen.'

Not at all. She began to tell him (again) how the two biggest departures in her life were leaving her family to study medicine and leaving her husband to live in France. She had come to the conclusion that she was not satiated with love for Peter Sheridan and exchanged a respectable life of unhappiness for the unrespectable unhappiness of being a woman who had cut her ties with love. Now it seemed, staring at her companion, whose voice was shaking all over the place, that in his damaged heart (too many cigarettes) he wanted to tie the knot, to close the circle of his life alone, which frankly was an affront.

It reminded her of the time they were walking on the beach in Villefranche and saw a wedding taking place in the harbour. The bridesmaids were dressed in yellow taffeta and the bride in cream and yellow satin. She had scoffed out loud, but what did the hippy Jurgen say?

'Give them a chance.'

This was the same man who only a few months before had told his girlfriend that nothing had taught him marriage was a good idea. She didn't believe him and took him to an Argentinian barbecue to propose to him. Great piles of scented wood. Hunks of beef from the pampas thrown on to the fire. His girlfriend ate her way through the red meat until she noticed Jurgen was not eating and remembered he was a militant vegetarian. Perhaps she had laughed too loudly when he told her that.

'I think Kitty Finch wants to harm me.'

'*Ach, nein.*' Jurgen frowned as if he was in pain. 'The Ket she only harms herself. Claude asked me why Madame Jacobs insisted she stay. But I have no idea why.'

She gazed at her friend with her cloudy, short-sighted eyes. 'I believe she wants the beautiful mad girl to distract her husband so she can finally leave him.'

Jurgen suddenly wanted to buy the accordion player a drink. He called the waiter and told him to offer the man in the big suit a beer. Madeleine watched the waiter whisper in the musician's ear and tried to forget how she came across Kitty Finch in the tunnel by the flower market in Cours Saleya four months ago. Their encounter was one more thing she wanted to add to the long list of things she wanted to forget.

She had found the flame-haired English girl on a cool spring morning on her way to buy two slabs of Marseilles soap, one made from palm oil, the other from olive oil, both mixed with sea plants from the Mediterranean by the local soap master. Kitty was naked and talking to herself on a box of rotten plums the farmers had thrown out at the end of the day. The homeless men who slept in the tunnel were laughing at her, making lewd remarks about her naked body. When Madeleine Sheridan asked her what had happened to her clothes, she said they were on the beach. Madeleine offered to drive to the beach and get her clothes for her. Kitty could stay exactly where she was and wait for her. And then she'd drive her back to the tourist villa where she was staying to study mountain plants. She often stayed there when Rita Dwighter had not let it out to retired hedge-fund managers because Kitty's mother used to clean for her. Mrs Finch was Rita Dwighter's right-hand woman, her secretary and cook but mostly her cleaner, because her right hand always had a mop in it.

Kitty Finch insisted she go away or she would shout for the police. Madeleine Sheridan could have left her there, but she did not do that. Kitty was too young to be talking to herself among the dead-eyed men staring at her breasts. To her surprise, the crazy girl suddenly changed her mind. Apparently she had left her jeans and a T-shirt and a pair of shoes, her favourite red polka-dot shoes, on the beach opposite the Hotel Negresco. Kitty leaned towards her and whispered in her ear, 'Fanks. I'll wait here while you get them.' Madeleine Sheridan had walked round the corner and when she thought Kitty could no longer see her she called an ambulance.

In her view Katherine Finch was suffering from psychic anxiety, loss of weight, reduced sleep, agitation, suicidal thoughts, pessimism about the future, impaired concentration.

The musician raised his glass of beer in a thank-you gesture to the snake-hipped man sitting with the old woman.

Kitty Finch had survived her summary. Her mother took her

home to Britain and she spent two months in a hospital in Kent, the Garden of England. Apparently the nurses were from Lithuania, Odessa and Kiev. In their white uniforms they looked like snowdrops on the mown green lawns of the hospital. That was what Kitty Finch told her mother and what Mrs Finch told Madeleine, who was astonished to learn that the nurses all chain-smoked in their lunch break.

Jurgen nudged her with his elbow. The accordion player from Marseilles was playing a tune for her. She felt too agitated to listen. Kitty had survived and now she had come to punish her. Perhaps even kill her. Why else was she here? She did not think Kitty was a safe person to drive Nina to the beach and up dangerous mountain roads. She should tell Isabel Jacobs that but somehow she couldn't bring herself to have that conversation. If she had been on her way to buy soap and ended up calling an ambulance, Transport Sanitaire in French, she did not feel her hands were entirely clean. All the same, to be naked in a public place, to be jumping forwards and then backwards while chanting something incoherent, this had made her frightened for the wretched young woman. It was impossible to believe that someone did not want to be saved from their incoherence.

When the accordion player nodded at Jurgen, the caretaker knew he was in luck. He would buy some hashish and he and Claude would smoke it and get out of the Riviera while all the tourists wanted to get into it. He put his purple sunglasses on again and told Madeleine Sheridan that he was very, very happy today but he was also a little tight in the bowels. He thought his colon was blocked and this was because he had not lived his dream. What was his dream? He took a sip of Pepsi and noticed the English doctor had dressed up for lunch. She had put lipstick on and her hair, what was left of it, had been washed and curled. He could not tell her his dream was to win the lotto and marry Kitty Ket.

TUESDAY

Reading and Writing

Joe Jacobs lay on his back in the master bedroom, as it was described in the villa's fact sheet, longing for a curry. The place he most wanted to be at this moment was in his Hindu tailor's workshop in Bethnal Green. Surrounded by silk. Drinking sweet tea. What he was missing in the Alpes-Maritimes was dhal. Rice. Yoghurt. And buses. He missed the top deck of buses. And newspapers. And weather forecasts. Sometimes he sat in his study in west London with the radio on and listened intently to what the weather was going to be like in Scotland, Ireland and Wales. If the sun was shining in west London, it comforted him to know it would be snowing in Scotland and raining in Wales. Now he was going to have to sit up and not lie down. Worse, he was going to have to stand up and search the master bedroom for Kitty Finch's poem. In the distance he could hear Mitchell shooting rabbits in the orchard. He knelt on the floor and grabbed the envelope he had kicked under the bed. He held the battered envelope in his hands and found himself staring at the title written in the neat scientific handwriting of a botanist used to making precise drawings of plants and labelling them.

Swimming Home

by

Kitty Finch

When he finally prised out the sheet of paper inside it, he was surprised to feel his hand trembling in the way his father's hand might have trembled if he had lived long enough to mend kettles in his old age. He held the page closer to his eyes and forced himself to read the words floating on the page. And then he moved the page further away from his eyes and read it again. There was no angle that made it easier to comprehend. Her words were all over the place, swimming round the edges of the rectangle of paper, sometimes disappearing altogether but coming back to the centre of the lined page with its sad and final message. What did she hope he might say to her after he had read it? He was mystified. A fish van had pulled up outside the villa. The voice bellowing through a loudspeaker was shouting out the names of fish. Some were *grand*, some were *petit*. Some were six francs and some were thirteen francs. None of them had swum home. They were all caught on the way. The Sellotape that had sealed the lip of the envelope reminded him of a plaster on a graze. He took a deep breath and exhaled slowly. He was going to have to busk it at lunch with her. He checked the inside of his jacket pocket to make sure his wallet was there and kicked the envelope under the bed, telling himself once again how much he hated Tuesdays. And Wednesdays, Thursdays, Fridays, etc.

et cetera

A Latin expression meaning 'and other things' or 'so forth' or 'the rest of such things'. The poem, 'Swimming Home', was mostly made up of etcs; he had counted seven of them in one half of the page alone. What kind of language was this?

> My mother says I'm the only jewel in her crown
> But I've made her tired with all my etc,
> So now she walks with sticks

To accept her language was to accept that she held him, her reader, in great esteem. He was being asked to make something of it and what he made of it was that every etc concealed some thing that could not be said.

Kitty was waiting for him on the terrace of Claude's café. To his displeasure he noticed that Jurgen was sitting at the table opposite her. He seemed to be playing with a piece of string, weaving it between his fingers to make a spider's web. It was becoming clear to him that Jurgen was a sort of guard dog to Kitty Finch, not exactly baring his teeth at all intruders but he was protective and possessive all the same. He seemed to have forgotten that it was she who was the intruder. All the same Jurgen was obviously there to make sure anyone who came near her was a welcome visitor and not a trespasser. He did not seem to elicit much affection from her. It was as if she knew he must never be patted and cuddled and made to feel anything less than alert on her behalf.

'Hi, Joe.' Kitty smiled. Her forehead looked as if she had pressed it against a hot iron. She was a redhead and the sun had been brutal to her pale skin.

He nodded, jangling the coins in his jacket pocket as he sat down. 'You should use sun block, Kitty,' he said paternally.

Claude, who knew he looked more like Mick Jagger every day and worked quite hard on this happy genetic accident, strutted to their table carrying a large bottle of mineral water and two glasses. Joe saw this as an opportunity to pass some time and avoid talking about the poem he had kicked under his bed with the cockroaches, etc.

He turned to Kitty. 'Did you order this?'

She shook her head and made a glum face at Claude. Joe heard himself bellowing at the pouting waiter.

'What's wrong with tap water?'

Claude stared at him with blatant dislike. 'Tap water is full of hormones.'

'No, it's not. Bottled water is a trick to get more money from tourists.'

Joe could hear Claude laughing. The only other sound was the birds. And the nervous hum inside Kitty Finch, who was a bird or something fairyish anyway. He couldn't look at her. Instead he fixed his eyes on Claude.

'Tell me, sir. Is your country incapable of processing water that is safe to drink?'

Claude, with the flourish of a low-rent pimp showing off his new diamond cufflinks, unscrewed the cap on the ice-cold bottle of water and walked towards his dogs, who were sleeping under the chestnut tree. He winked at Jurgen as he poured the water into the chipped ceramic bowls that lay by their paws. The dogs lapped at the water indifferently and then gave up. Claude patted their heads and strutted back into the café. When he came out again he was holding a glass of warm cloudy tap water, which he handed to the English poet.

Joe held the glass up to the sun. 'I assume,' he shouted to the caretaker, who was still untangling his string, 'that this glass of water comes from a putrid swamp.' He gulped the water down in one go and pointed to the empty glass. 'This is water. It can be found in oceans and polar ice caps . . . It can be found in clouds and rivers . . . it will . . .'

Claude snapped his fingers under the poet's nose. 'Thank you, monsieur, for the geography lesson. But what we want to know is have you read the poetry of our friend here?' He pointed to Kitty. 'Because she tells us you are a very respected poet and she says you have so kindly offered to give her an opinion.'

Joe had to finally look at Kitty Finch. Her grey eyes that were sometimes green seemed to shine with extra radiance in her sunburnt face. She did not seem in the least embarrassed by Claude's intervention on her behalf. In fact she appeared to be amused, even grateful. Joe reckoned this was the worst day of his holiday so far. He was too old, too busy to have to endure a village full of idiots more fascinated with him than he was with them.

'That is a private conversation between two writers,' he said quietly to no one in particular.

Kitty blushed and stared at her feet. 'Do you think I'm a writer?'

Joe frowned. 'Yeah, I think you probably are.'

He stared nervously at Jurgen, who appeared to be lost in the puzzle of his string. The dogs were now lapping up the expensive bottled water in their bowls. Claude danced into the café, where he had pinned up a poster of Charlie Chaplin standing white-faced in a circle of light, his walking stick between his legs. Underneath it were the words *Les Temps modernes*. Next to it stood the new rubber model of ET, his baby alien neck garlanded with a string of fake plastic ivy. He started to fry yesterday's potatoes in duck fat, peering out of the window to see what the poet and Kitty Ket were up to.

Kitty leaned forward and touched Joe's shoulder with her hand. It was a strange gesture. As if she were testing that he was there.

'I've got all your books in my room.'

She sounded vaguely threatening. As if by owning his books, he in turn owed her something. The copper curls of her long unbrushed hair falling over her shoulders resembled a marvellous dream he might have invented to cheer himself up. How had she managed to hog so much beauty? She smelt of roses. She was soft and slender and supple. She was interesting and lovely. She loved plants. She had green fingers. And more literally, green fingernails. She admired him, wanted his attention and intrigued him, but he need not have bothered to read her poem because he understood it already.

Claude, with new humility and even-handedness, placed a bowl of green salad and fried potatoes on their table. Joe picked up a potato and dipped it in mustard.

'I've been thinking about your title, "Swimming Home".'

His tone was offhand, more nonchalant than he felt. He did not tell her how he had been thinking about her title. The rectangular swimming pool that had been carved from stone in the grounds of the villa reminded him of a coffin. A floating open coffin lit with the underwater lights Jurgen swore at when he fiddled with the incandescent light bulbs he'd had to change twice since they arrived. A swimming pool was just a hole in the ground. A grave filled with water.

Two paragliders drifted on yellow silk between the mountains. The narrow cobbled streets of the village were deserted. The paragliders were landing near the river instead of the usual base five kilometres away.

Kitty stuffed her mouth with lettuce leaves. A thin cat purred against her ankles as she threw her potato chips under the table. She leaned forward.

'Something happened to me this year. I've forgotten things.' She frowned and he saw that the burn on her forehead was beginning to blister.

'What sort of things?'

'I can't rah rah rah rah rah.'

She was not a poet. She was a poem. She was about to snap in half. He thought his own poetry had made her la la la la love him. It was unbearable. He could not bear it. She was still trying to remember how to say remember.

If he couldn't talk about her poem what good was he? He might as well move to the countryside and run the tombola stand at the church fête. He might as well take up writing stories set in the declining years of empire featuring a dusty black Humber V8 Snipe with an aged loyal driver.

She was an astute reader and she was troubled and she had suicidal thoughts, but then what did he want his readers to be like? Were they required to eat all their vegetables, have a regular monthly salary and pension fund with yearly gym membership and a loyalty card to their favourite supermarket?

Her gaze, the adrenalin of it was like a stain, the etcs in her poem a bright light, a high noise. And if all this wasn't terrifying enough, her attention to the detail of every day was even more so, to pollen and struggling trees and the instincts of animals, to the difficulties of pretending to be relentlessly sane, to the way he walked (he had kept the rheumatism that aged him a secret from his family), to the nuance of mood and feeling in them all. Yesterday he had watched her free some bees trapped in the glass of a lantern as if it were she who was held captive. She was as receptive as it was possible to be, an explorer, an adventurer, a nightmare. Every moment with her was a kind of emergency, her words always too direct, too raw, too truthful.

There was nothing for it but to lie.

'I'm sorry, Kitty, but I haven't read your poem yet. AND I

have a deadline with my publisher. AND I have to give a reading in Kraków in three weeks. AND I promised to take Nina fishing this afternoon.'

'Right.' She bit her lip and looked away. 'Right,' she said again, but her voice was breaking. Jurgen seemed to have disappeared and Kitty was biting her fingers.

'Why don't you give it to Jurgen to read?' As soon as he said it he wished he hadn't. She was literally changing colour in front of him. It was not so much a blush as a fuse. An electrical cable wire starting to melt. She fixed him with a glare of such intense hostility he wondered what it was he had actually done that was so bad.

'My poem is a conversation with you and no one else.'

It shouldn't be happening, his search for love in her, but it was. He would go to the ends of the earth to find love. He was trying not to, but the more he tried not to search, the more there was to find. He could see her on a British beach with a Thermos of tea in her bag, dodging the cold waves, tracing her name in the sand, looking out at the nuclear power stations built in the distance. This was more her landscape, a catastrophic poem in itself. He had touched her with his words, but he knew he must not touch her in any other sort of way, in a more literal way, with his lips for example. That would be taking advantage. He had to fight it all the way. The way to where? He didn't know, but he would fight it to the very end. If he were religious he would get down on his knees and pray. Father, take all this away. Away. Let all this fade away. He knew it was as much a plea or a wish or a chant to his own father, the sombre bearded patriarch, the shadow he had chased all his life, etc. His father said goodbye, etc. His mother said goodbye, etc. He hid in a dark forest in western Poland, etc.

Kitty stood up and fumbled with her purse. He told her not to worry. Please. He wanted to buy her lunch. She insisted she would pay her share. He saw her purse was flat, empty, there was nothing in it but she was searching for coins all the same. He insisted. It meant nothing to him. Please would she leave the bill for him to sort out? She was shouting too while her fingers frantically searched inside the purse, shouting at him to shut up shut up shut up, who did he think she was, what was he thinking she was? Blushing and furious, she at last found what she had been looking for, a grubby twenty-franc note folded in two as if it had been saved for something. She unfolded it carefully, her hands shaking as she slid it under a saucer, and then she ran down one of the cobbled streets. He could hear her coughing. And then he heard Jurgen's voice talking to her and realised the caretaker must have been waiting for her. She was asking him in French why the pool was so cloudy and he was asking her why she was crying. He heard Jurgen say forget forget, the sun is shining, Kitty Ket. It was a sort of song: forget forget Kitty Ket forget forget Kitty Ket.

Joe searched for his silk handkerchief and buried his face in it. Silk was used to make early bulletproof vests. It was a second skin and he needed it. What was he supposed to do? What was he supposed to do with her poem? He was not her doctor. She didn't want him to shine a light in her eyes. Should he tell Isabel the young woman she had invited to stay had threatened to do something?

He would be in Poland soon. Performing in an old palace in Kraków. His translator and guide would talk him through tram routes and menus. She would take him to rest in the Tatra Mountains and show him the wooden dachas built in the forest. Women in headscarves would tend their geese and invite him to taste their jams and cheeses. When he finally departed from Warsaw airport and customs asked him if he was taking any caviar out of the country, he would say, 'No caviar. I'm taking my black oily past out of the country and it belongs to us both. It goes like this. My father said goodbye, etc. My mother said goodbye, etc. They hid me in a dark forest in western Poland, etc.'

Someone was patting his shoulder. To his surprise, Claude had placed a glass of cold lager on his table. What had brought on this kind fraternal gesture from the Mick Jagger of Wurzelshire? Joe drank it down in one long thirsty gulp. He picked up the note Kitty had left under the saucer and poked it into his shirt pocket before Claude swept it up to pay his hair stylist. He would find a way of returning it to her. She was going in two days' time, thank God. It would be over. To his dismay, just as he was beginning to feel elated at being on his own, he saw his daughter walking down the hill towards the café.

Nina was carrying a fishing net and a bucket. Oh no.

Bloody hell. He began to moan to himself. Here she is. My daughter is wearing mascara to go fishing. And earrings. Big gold hoops that will be caught on the branches of trees. Now he would have to hike with her all the way to the river in the afternoon heat as he had promised her. Two kilometres.

No one seemed to understand he was fifty-seven years old. He would have to scramble down the slope of the river bank and try not to slip on the stones. He waved unenthusiastically and his daughter shook the fishing net in his direction. When she finally slumped down on the chair opposite him, he took her hand and squeezed it. 'Congratulations. Your mother told me you've started your period at last.'

'Shut the fuck up.' Nina rolled her eyes and stared in rapt fascination at the bucket.

'OK, I will. Why don't we cancel fishing and just sit here and drink lager together?'

'No way.'

Joe cleared his throat. 'Um . . . have you got everything you need . . . you know, for a girl who has just started . . .?'

'Shut up.'

'OK, I will.'

'Where's Kitty?'

'She's . . . um . . . I don't know where she's gone.'

Nina stared at her father's hair. He had actually brushed it for a change. She had to admit he was quite handsome even though he was repulsive. He had made an effort to look good for Kitty whatever he said.

'Did you like her poem?'

What was he supposed to say? Again he did what he did

best, which was to lie.

'I haven't read it yet.'

Nina punched his arm as hard as she could.

'She was so nervous about you reading it she nearly crashed the car. With ME in it. She practically drove us both over the mountains. She had to summon all her courage to see you. She was SHAKING.'

'Oh, God.' Joe blew out his cheeks.

'Why "Oh, GOD"? I thought you didn't believe in God?' his daughter snarled and turned her back on him.

He banged the table and it jumped.

'Don't EVER get into a car with Kitty Finch again. Do you understand?'

Nina thought she sort of understood but didn't really know what it was she had agreed to understand. Was Kitty a bad driver or what? Her father looked furious.

'I can't stand THE DEPRESSED. It's like a job, it's the only thing they work hard at. Oh good my depression is very well today. Oh good today I have another mysterious symptom and I will have another one tomorrow. The DEPRESSED are full of hate and bile and when they are not having panic attacks they are writing poems. What do they want their poems to DO? Their depression is the most VITAL thing about them. Their poems are threats. ALWAYS threats. There is no sensation that is keener or more active than their pain. They give nothing back except their depression. It's just another utility. Like electricity and water and gas and democracy. They could not survive without it. GOD, I'M SO THIRSTY. WHERE'S CLAUDE?'

Claude poked his head round the door. He was trying not to laugh but looked at Joe with slightly more respect than usual. In fact he was thinking about asking him in confidence if he might see his way to paying the tab Mitchell was running up in the café.

'Please, Claude, bring me some water. Any water. A bottle will do. No. I'll have another beer. A large one. Don't you do pints in this country?'

Claude nodded and disappeared inside the café, where he had switched on the television to watch the football. Nina picked up the fishing net and waved it in her father's face.

'The whole point of this afternoon is we are going fishing, so stand up and start walking, because you are boring me shitless.'

Shitless was her newest word and she said it with relish.

'I know I don't bore you "shitless",' her father growled pathetically, his voice now hoarse.

Nina did not dare say it again because every time he took her out with the net and bucket she was always excited at the horrors he somehow managed to scoop up.

Claude brought out the beer, 'a large one', in a pint glass and explained to Nina that he was taking no more orders from her father because he was watching the semi between Sweden and Brazil.

'Fair enough.' Joe threw some money on the table and when Claude whispered something in his ear, he slapped a bundle of notes into his hand and told him he would pay for anything Mitchell ordered at the café but he must not know, the fat man must not be told that his endless pastries would be paid for with the royalties of the rich arsehole poet.

Claude tapped his nose. Their plan was safe with him. He glanced at Nina and then snapped a branch of the purple bougainvillea growing up the wall. He looped the flowers into a bracelet and offered it to her with a small bow. 'For the beautiful daughter of the poet.'

Nina found herself brazenly holding out her arm so he could wrap the violet petals around it like a handcuff. Her pulse was going berserk as his fingertips touched her wrist.

'Give me the net, Nina.' Her father held out his arm. 'I can use it to poke my eyes out. Actually I would like to watch the World Cup with Claude. You need to learn to be a bit kinder to your father.'

She bit her lip in what she hoped was an appealing manner and dared herself to glance at Claude, who shrugged helplessly. They both knew he would rather just watch her.

As they walked past the church to get to the road that Joe knew led to the gate that led to the field of snorting bulls that led to the path that led to the bridge that led to the river, he felt his daughter's hand slip into his trouser pocket.

'Nearly there,' she said encouragingly.

'Shut up,' her father replied.

'I think you get depressed. Don't you, Dad?'

Joe stumbled on an uneven cobblestone.

'As you said, "We are nearly there."'

The Photograph

The group of Japanese tourists was happy. They had been smiling for what seemed an unnaturally long time. Isabel, who was sitting in the shade of a silver olive tree waiting for Laura, reckoned they had been smiling for about twenty minutes. They were taking photographs of each other outside the faded pink château of the Matisse Museum and their smiles were beginning to look pained and tormented.

The park was full of families picnicking under the olive trees. Four old men playing *boules* in the shade paused their game to talk about the heatwave that was ruining the vineyards in France. Laura was waving to her and did not realise she had walked straight into a photograph. The seven Japanese tourists standing with their arms draped around each other were still smiling, Laura in front of them, her arm raised in the air as the camera flashed.

Isabel had always been first in class to raise her hand at her grammar school in Cardiff. She had known the answers long before the other girls caught up, girls who, like her, all wore green blazers inscribed with the school motto, Let Knowledge Serve the World. Now she thought she would change the school motto to something that warned the girls that knowledge would not necessarily serve them, nor would it make them happy. There was a chance it would instead throw light on visions they did not want to see. The new motto would have to take into account the idea that knowledge was sometimes hard to live with and once the clever young girls of Cardiff had a taste for it they would never be able to put the genie back in the bottle.

The men had resumed their game of *boules*. Voices from a radio somewhere close by were discussing the air controllers' strike. Flasks of coffee were being opened under the trees. Children fell off their bicycles. Families unpacked sandwiches and fruit. Isabel could see the sweep of white and blue belle époque hotels built on the hill and knew that somewhere nearby was the cemetery where Matisse was buried. Laura was holding a bottle of red wine in her left hand. Isabel called out to her, but Laura had seen her anyway. She was a fast walker, efficient and focused. Laura would have things to say about her inviting Kitty Finch to stay, but Isabel would insist she pay the entire summer's rent for the villa herself. Laura and Mitchell must book themselves into a country hotel near Cannes she had read about in a guidebook. A yellow ochre Provençal manor that served fine wines and sea bass in a crust of salt. This would be the right place for Mitchell, who had been hoping for an epic gastronomic summer but instead found himself unwillingly sharing his holiday with a stranger who seemed to be starving herself. Laura and Mitchell thrived on order and structure. Mitchell made five-year plans for their business in Euston, flow charts describing tasks to be done, the logic of decisions, the outcomes desired. She admired their faith in the future: the belief that it delivered outcomes that could be organised to come out in the right shape.

Laura was smiling but she did not look happy. She sat down

beside Isabel and took off her sandals. And then she pulled at tufts of the parched grass with her fingers and told her friend that the shop in Euston was closing down. She and Mitchell could no longer make ends meet. They could barely pay their mortgage. They had come to France with five credit cards between them and not very much cash. They could not even afford to buy petrol for the Mercedes Mitchell had foolishly hired at the airport. In fact Mitchell had run up debts she was only just beginning to get a grip on. He owed large sums of money all over the place. For months he had been saying something would turn up, but nothing had turned up. The shop would go into liquidation. When they returned to London they would have to sell their house.

Isabel moved closer to Laura and put her arms around her. Laura was so tall it was sometimes hard to believe she was not literally above the things that bothered everyone else. She was obviously not feeling herself, because her shoulders were pulled down too. Her friend had never adopted the stoop tall people sometimes develop to make themselves human scale, but now she looked crushed.

'Let's open the wine.' Laura had forgotten to bring a corkscrew so they used the end of Isabel's comb, plunging its long plastic spike into the cork, and found themselves drinking from the bottle, passing it to each other like teenagers on their first holiday away from family. Isabel told Laura how she had spent the morning searching shops for sanitary towels for Nina, but had no idea how to say it in French. At last the man in the pharmacy told her the words were '*serviettes hygiéniques*'. He had wrapped the pads in a brown paper bag and then in a plastic bag and then in another plastic bag as if in his mind they were already soaked in blood. And then she changed the subject. She wanted to know if Laura had a personal bank account. Laura shook her head. She and Mitchell had had a joint account ever since they set up business together. And then Laura changed the subject and asked Isabel if she thought Kitty Finch might be a little . . . she searched for the word . . . 'touched'? The word stuck in her mouth and she wished she had another language to translate what she meant, because the only words stored inside her were from the school playground of her generation, a lexicon that in no particular order started with barmy, bonkers, barking and went on to loopy, nuts, off with the fairies and then danced up the alphabet again to end with cuckoo. Laura began to tell her how much Kitty's arrival alarmed her. Just as she was leaving the villa to drive to the Matisse Museum she had seen Kitty arrange the tails of three rabbits Mitchell had shot in the orchard in a vase – as if they were flowers. The thing was, she must have actually cut the tails off the rabbits herself. With a knife. She must have sawed through the rabbits with a carving knife. Isabel did not reply because she was writing Laura a cheque. Peering over her shoulder, Laura saw it was for a considerable amount of money and was signed in Isabel's maiden name.

Isabel Rhys Jones. When they were students introducing themselves to each other in the bar, Isabel always pronounced her home city in Welsh: Caerdydd. She had had a Welsh accent to start with and then it more or less disappeared. In the second year of their studies Isabel spoke with an English accent that wasn't quite English but would become so by the time she was on television reporting from Africa. Laura, who had studied African languages, tried to not sound English when she spoke Swahili. It was a complicated business and she would have liked to think about it some more, but Isabel had put the lid back on her pen and was clearing her throat. She was saying something and she sounded quite Welsh. Laura missed the first bit of what her friend was saying but tuned in on time to hear how the North African cleaner who mopped the floors for a pittance in the villa was apparently on strike. The woman wore a headscarf and mended the European plugs for Jurgen, who had gleefully discovered she was more skilled with electrics than he was. Laura had seen her gazing at the wires and then out of the window at the silver light that apparently cured Matisse's tuberculosis. This woman had been on her mind for some reason and just as she was wondering why she had been so preoccupied by her she remembered what Isabel had said when she was writing out the cheque. It was something to do with Laura opening a separate account from the one she shared with Mitchell. She started to laugh and reminded Isabel that her maiden name was Laura Cable.

The Thing

'You shouldn't cover yourself with so much sun lotion, Mitchell.'

Kitty Finch was obviously upset about something. She had taken off all her clothes and stood naked at the edge of the pool as if no one else was there. 'It changes the chemical balance of the water.'

Mitchell put a protective hand on the dome of his stomach and groaned.

'The water is actually CLOUDY.' Kitty sounded furious. She ran around the sides of the pool staring into it from every angle. 'Jurgen has got the chemical treatment all wrong.' She stamped her bare foot on the hot paving stones. 'It's chemistry that does the fine-tuning. He's added chlorine tablets to the skimmer box and now it's too concentrated in the deep end.'

Once again Mitchell took it upon himself to tell her to fuck off. Why didn't she make herself a cheese sandwich and go and get lost in the woods? In fact he would even drive her there if she could see her way to putting some petrol in his Mercedes.

'You're so easily frightened, Mitchell.'

She jumped towards him. Two long leaps as if she was playing at being a gazelle or a deer and was taunting him to come and hunt her down. Her ribs poked out of her skin like the wires of the trap Mitchell had bought for the rat.

'It's a good thing Laura's so tall, isn't it? She can peer

over your head when you shoot animals and never have to look at the ground where they lie wounded.'

Kitty leapt into the cloudy water holding her nose. Mitchell sat up and immediately felt dizzy. The sun always made him ill. Next year he would suggest they hire a chalet on the edge of an icy fjord in Norway, as far away from the Jacobs family as possible. He would catch seals and thrash himself with birch twigs in saunas and then he'd run out into the snow and scream while Laura practised speaking Yoruba and longed for Africa.

'THE WATER IS FUCKED.'

What had got into her? Adjusting the umbrella over his pink bald head, he could see Joe limping towards the small gate that led to the back of the garden. Nina followed him through the cypress trees carrying a red bucket and a net.

'Hi, Joe.'

Kitty jumped out of the pool and started to shake water out of the copper coils of her hair. He nodded at her, relieved that despite their unpleasant meeting earlier she sounded genuinely pleased to see him. He pointed to the bucket Nina was carrying with some difficulty to the edge of the pool.

'Come and see what we found in the river.'

They crowded around the bucket, which was half full of muddy water. A slimy grey creature with a red stripe down its spine clung to a clump of weed. It was as thick as Mitchell's thumb and seemed to have some sort of pulse because the water trembled above it. Every now and again it curled into a ball and slowly straightened out again.

'What is it?' Mitchell couldn't believe they had bothered to lug this vile creature across the fields all the way back to the villa.

'It's a thing.' Joe smirked.

Mitchell groaned and moved away. 'Nasty.'

'Dad always finds gross things.'

Nina stared over Kitty's shoulder, making sure not to look at her breasts, which were now hanging over the bucket as she peered in. She didn't want to look at naked Kitty Finch and her father standing too near her. Nina could count the bones that ran like beads down her spine. Kitty was a starver. Her room was full of rotting food she had hidden under cushions. As far as Nina was concerned, she'd rather stare at the blotches of chewing gum on London pavement than at her father and Kitty Finch.

Kitty reached for a towel. She was all fingers and thumbs, dropping it and picking it up again until Joe finally took it from her and helped wrap it around her waist.

'What do you think it is?' Kitty stared into the bucket.

'It's a creepy-crawly,' Joe announced. 'My best find yet.'

Nina thought it might be a centipede. It had hundreds of tiny legs that were frantically waving around in the water, trying to find something to grip on to.

'What exactly is it you are looking for when you go fishing?' Kitty lowered her voice, as if the creature might hear her. 'Do you find the things you want to find?'

'What are you talking about?' Mitchell sounded like a schoolteacher irritated with a child.

'Don't talk to her like that.' Joe's arms were now clasped

around Kitty's waist, holding up the towel as if his life depended on it.

'She's asking why don't I find silver fish and pretty shells? The answer is they are there anyway.'

While he talked he poked his finger through the wet curls of Kitty's hair. Nina saw her mother and Laura walking through the white gate. Her father let go of the towel and Kitty blushed. Nina stared miserably into the cypress trees, pretending to look for the hedgehog she knew sheltered in the garden. Joe walked over to the plastic recliner and lay down. He glanced at his wife, who had walked over to the bucket. There were leaves in her hair and grass stains on her bare shins. She had not so much distanced herself from him as moved out to another neighbourhood altogether. There was new vigour in the way she stood by the bucket. Her determination not to love him seemed to have renewed her energy.

Mitchell was still peering at the creature crawling up the sides of the red plastic bucket. It was perfectly camouflaged by the red markings on its spine.

'What are you going to do with your slug?'

Everyone looked at Joe.

'Yes,' he said. 'My "thing" is freaking you all out. Let's put it on a leaf in the garden.'

'No.' Laura squirmed. 'It'll only make its way back here.'

'Or crawl through the plughole and come up in the water.' Mitchell looked truly alarmed.

Laura shuddered and then screamed, 'It's climbing out. It's nearly out.' She ran to the bucket and threw a towel over it.

'Do something to stop it, Joe.'

Joe limped to the bucket, removed the towel and flicked the creature back into the bottom of the water with his thumb.

'It is really quite tiny.' He yawned. 'It's just a strange tiny slimy thing.'

A clump of river weed trailed down his eyebrow. Everything had gone very quiet. Even the late-afternoon rasp of the cicadas seemed to have faded away. When Joe opened his eyes, everyone except Laura had disappeared into the villa. Laura was shaking but her voice was matter of fact.

'Look, I know Isabel invited Kitty to stay.' She stopped and started again. 'But you don't have to. I mean, do you? Do you have to? Do you? Do you have to keep doing it?'

Joe clenched his fists inside his pockets.

'Doing what?'

WEDNESDAY

Body Electric

Jurgen and Claude were smoking the hashish Jurgen had bought from the accordion player on the beach in Nice. He usually bought it from the driver who dropped the immigrant cleaners at the tourist villas, but they were organising a strike. What's more the news last night forecast a gale and the entire village had spent the night preparing for it. Jurgen's cottage was owned by Rita Dwighter but not yet 'restored' and he wanted to keep it that way. Sometimes he threw heavy objects at the walls in the hope that it would become unrestorable and keep its status as the ugly dysfunctional child in Rita Dwighter's family of properties.

Now he was huddled over Claude's mobile phone. Claude had recorded a cow mooing. He didn't know why, but he had to do it. He had walked into a field and held his phone as close as he dared to the cow's mouth. If Jurgen pressed the play button the cow mooed. Technology had made the cow sound familiar but uncomfortably strange as well. Every time the cow mooed they laughed hysterically, because the cow had trodden on Claude's big toe and now his toenail was deformed.

Madame Dwighter had told Jurgen to wait in for her call. Jurgen didn't mind. Waiting in made a change from being called out to change a light bulb in the 'Provençal style' villas he would never afford to buy. A pile of Picasso prints he had bought in a job lot at the flea market lay against the wall. He preferred the rubber model of ET he had found for Claude. Rita Dwighter had instructed him to frame and hang 'the Picassos' in every available space left in the three villas she owned, but he couldn't be bothered. It was more interesting hearing the cow mooing on Claude's mobile.

When Jurgen started to roll another joint he could hear a telephone ringing. Claude pointed to the telephone lying on the floor. Jurgen twisted his nose with his thumb and forefinger and eventually picked up the receiver.

Claude had to slap his hand over his mouth to stop himself from laughing as loudly as he would have liked. Jurgen didn't want to be a caretaker. Madame Dwighter was always asking him to tell her what was on his mind, but he only ever told Claude what was on his mind. There was only ever one thing on Jurgen's mind.

Kitty Finch. If pressed he would include: sex, drugs, Buddhism as a means to achieve oneness in life, no meat, no vivisection, Kitty Finch, no vaccination, no alcohol, Kitty Finch, purity of body and soul, herbal remedies, playing slide guitar, Kitty Finch, becoming what Jack Kerouac described as a Nature Boy Saint. He heard his friend telling Madame

Dwighter that yes, everything was very serene in the villa this year. Yes, the famous English poet and his family were enjoying their vacation. In fact they had a surprise visitor. Mademoiselle Finch was staying in the spare room and she was charming them all. Yes, she had very good equilibrium this year and she had written something to show the poet.

Claude unbuttoned his jeans and let them fall to his knees. Jurgen had to hold the phone away from his ear while he doubled over, making obscene gestures to Claude, who was now doing press-ups in his Calvin Klein boxer shorts on the floor. Jurgen tapped the joint against his knee and continued speaking to Rita Dwighter, who was phoning from tax exile in Spain. He would soon have to call her *Señora*.

Yes, the fact sheet was up to date. Yes, the water in the pool was perfect. Yes, the cleaners were doing a good job. Yes, he had replaced the broken window. Yes, he was feeling good in himself. Yes, the heatwave was coming to an end. Yes, there were going to be thunderstorms. Yes, everyone knew about the weather forecast. Yes, he would secure the shutters.

Claude could hear the voice of Rita Dwighter fall out of the receiver and disappear into the clouds of hashish smoke. Everyone in the village laughed at the mention of the wealthy psychoanalyst and property developer who paid Jurgen so handsomely for his lack of skill. They liked to joke that she had built a helicopter pad for businessmen to land outside her consulting room in west London. They sat on designer chairs while their pilots, usually former alcoholics struck off by the commercial airlines, smoked duty-free cigarettes in the rain. Claude had been thinking of spreading a rumour that one of her most affluent clients had managed to get his arm stuck in the blades of the propeller just as she had sorted out why he liked to dress up in a Nazi uniform and whip prostitutes. He had had to have his arm amputated and stopped seeing her, which meant she could not afford to buy the postman's cottage after all.

When Madame Dwighter came to inspect her properties, which to Jurgen's relief was not often, she always invited Claude with his Mick Jagger looks to supper. The last time he ate with her she stuck an erect pineapple stalk into a moist melting Brie and asked him to help himself.

Jurgen finally put the phone down. He stared at the Picasso prints as if he wanted to murder them. He told Claude, who had now taken off his T-shirt and was lying face down on the floor in his boxer shorts, that he'd been instructed to hang *Guernica* in the corridor to hide the jagged cracks in the plaster. Dominatrix Dwighter was obviously impressed by the techniques the great artist employed to say something about the human condition. Claude just about managed to stand up and put on one of Jurgen's battered CDs. It had been lying on top of an Indian jewellery box labelled 'Prague Muzic. Ket's Selection for Calm'.

Someone was knocking on the door. Jurgen disliked all visitors because they were always asking him to do his job. This time it was the pretty fourteen-year-old daughter of the arsehole British poet. She was wearing a short white skirt and naturally she wanted him to do something.

'My mother asked me to come over to check you'd booked the horse-riding for tomorrow.'

He nodded wisely, as if nothing else had ever been on his mind. 'Come in. Claude's here.'

When Jurgen said Claude's here, the CD seemed to jump or it got stuck or something happened. Nina heard a violin playing and under it the sound of a wolf howling and the female singer breathing a word that sounded like snowburst. She glanced at Claude, who was dancing in his boxer shorts. His back was so smooth and brown she stared at the wall instead.

'*Bonjour*, Nina. The dogs ate my jeans so now I only have my shorts. The CD is scratched but I like it for calming.'

When she looked through him pitifully, he saw himself as a snail crushed on the rope sole of her red espadrilles. Jurgen had his hands on his bony hips, his elbows pointing out in triangles. He seemed to want her opinion on his dreadlocks.

'So do you think I should cut off my hair?'

'Yeah.'

'I make my hair like this to be different from my father.'

He laughed and Claude laughed with him.

snowburst
drifting away
to the dark

Jurgen was trying to get a grip on geography. 'Austria is the start of my childhood. Then I think it was Baden-Baden. My father taught me to cut timber in the old tradition.' He scratched his head. 'I think it was Austrian. Something old anyway. So what kind of music do you like?'

'Nirvana is my favourite band.'

'Ah, you are liking the Kurt Cobain with his blue eyes, yes?'

She told him she had made a shrine to Kurt Cobain in her bedroom after he had shot himself that spring. April the fifth to be precise but his body was found on April the eighth. She had played his album *In Utero* all that day.

Jurgen cocked his dreadlocks to one side. 'Has your father read Kitty Ket's poem yet?'

'No. I'm going to read it myself.'

Claude pouted and strutted towards the fridge. 'That is a good plan. Do you want a beer?'

She shrugged. Claude was so anxious to please her it was pathetic. Claude translated her shrug as an enthusiastic Yes.

'I have to bring my own beer over to Jurgen's because he only drinks carrot juice.'

Jurgen had just heard a motorbike pull up outside his cottage. It was his friend Jean-Paul, who always gave him a commission on horse-riding bookings. Jean-Paul only kept ponies, so it was not exactly going to be a horse ride, but the ponies had hooves and a nice tail all the same. When he ran out of the door to make the deal, Claude reached for his T-shirt and struggled to put it on.

Nina stared at everything that wasn't him. And then she sat cross-legged on the floor, her back leaning against the wall, while he walked over with a beer in his hand. He opened it for her and sat down so close their thighs almost touched.

'So are you enjoying your vacation?'

She took a swig of the sour-tasting beer. 'It's OK.'

'If you come to my café I'll show you the Extra Terrestrial I keep in my kitchen.'

What was he talking about? She found herself moving closer to his shoulder. And then she turned her face towards him and she made her eyes say you can kiss me kiss me kiss me and there was a second when she sensed he wasn't sure what she meant. The beer was still in her hand and she put it down on the floor.

> drifting away
> to the dark
> forest

His lips were warm and they were on hers. She was kissing Mick Jagger and he was devouring her like a wolf or something fierce but soft as well and definitely not calm. He was telling her she was so so everything. She moved even closer and then he stopped talking.

> to the dark
> forest
> where trees bleed
> snowburst

When she peeped her eyes open and saw he had his eyes shut she shut her eyes again, but then the door opened and

Jurgen was standing in the middle of the room blinking at them.

'So everything is cool with the horse-riding.'

There was a kissing coma in the atmosphere. Everything had gone dark red. Jurgen put his hands on his hips so his elbows would jut out and the vibes could flow through the triangles his elbows made.

'Please, I am asking you to read the Ket's poem so you can tell me the way to her heart.'

THURSDAY

The Plot

Nina opened the door of her parents' bedroom and skated in her socks across the tiled floor. She was wearing socks despite the heat because her left foot was swollen from a bee sting. To give her courage for the task in hand she had spent the last hour smearing her eyelids with Kitty's blue stick of kohl. When she looked in the mirror her brown eyes were glittering and certain. From the window by the bed she could see her mother and Laura talking by the pool. Her father had gone to Nice to see the Russian Orthodox Cathedral and Kitty Finch was with Jurgen as usual. They were going to collect cow dung from the fields and then spread it over Jurgen's new allotment, which she said she had 'taken over for the summer'. No one could work out why she wasn't actually living with Jurgen in his cottage next door, but her mother had implied that Kitty might not be as 'sweet' on him as he was on her. She heard a bashing noise coming from the kitchen. Mitchell had wrapped a slab of dark chocolate in a tea cloth and was hammering at it excitedly. It was hot outside but she felt cold in her parents' room, as if it was an ice rink after all. She knew what the envelope looked like but she couldn't see it anywhere. What she needed was a torch, because she must not put the lights on and attract attention. If anyone came in she would slip into the bathroom and hide behind the door. On the table by her mother's side of the bed she noticed a slab of waxy honeycomb half wrapped in a page of newspaper. It had obviously been tied with the green string that lay next to it. She walked towards it and saw it was a gift from her father, because he had written in black ink across the page,

To my sweetest with my whole love as always, Jozef.

Nina frowned at the thick golden honey oozing through the holes. If her parents quite liked each other after all it would ruin the story she had put together for herself. When she thought about her parents, which was most of the time, she was always trying to fit the pieces together. What was the plot? Her father had very gentle hands and yesterday they were all over her mother. She had seen them kissing in the hallway like something out of a film, pulled into each other while moths crashed into the light bulb above their heads. As far as she was concerned, her parents tragically couldn't stand the sight of each other and only loved her. The plot was that her mother abandoned her only daughter to go and hug orphans in Romania. Tragically (so much tragedy) Nina had taken her mother's place in the family home and become her father's most precious companion, always second-guessing his moods and needs. But things started to wobble when her mother asked her if she'd like to go to a special restaurant by the sea for an ice cream with a sparkler in it. What's more, if her parents were kissing yesterday (the sheets on their unmade bed looked a bit frantic), and if they seemed to understand each other in a way that left her out, the plot was going off track.

It was only after six minutes of urgent searching that she eventually found the envelope with Kitty's poem inside it. She had given up rummaging through the silk shirts and handkerchiefs her father always ironed so carefully and crawled on her knees to look under the bed. When she saw the envelope propped up against her father's slippers and two dead brown cockroaches lying on their backs, she lay on her stomach and swept it up with her arm. There was something else under the bed too but she did not have time to find out what it was.

The window overlooking the pool was a problem. Her mother was sitting on the steps by the shallow end eating an apple. She could hear her asking Laura why she was learning Yoruba and Laura saying, 'Why not? Over twenty million people speak it.'

She crouched on the floor where she could not be seen and tore the Sellotape off the lip of the envelope. It was empty. She peered inside it. A sheet of paper had been folded into a square the size of a matchbox and it was stuck at the bottom of the envelope like an old shoe wedged into the mud of a river. She scooped it out and began carefully to unfold it.

Swimming Home

by

Kitty Finch

After she read it Nina didn't bother to fold the paper back into its intricate squares. She shoved it inside the envelope and put it back under the bed with the cockroaches. Why hadn't her father read it? He would understand exactly what was going on in Kitty's mind.

She made her way up the stairs to the open-plan living room and poked her head through the French doors.

Her mother was dangling her feet in the warm water and she was laughing. It made Nina frown because the sound was so rare. She found Mitchell frying liver in the kitchen. He was wearing one of his most flamboyant Hawaiian shirts to cook in.

'Hello,' he snorted. 'Have you come for a morsel?'

Nina leaned her back against the fridge and folded her arms.

'What have you done to your eyes?' Mitchell peered at the blue sparkling kohl smeared over her eyelids. 'Has someone punched your lights out?'

Nina took a deep breath to stop herself from screaming.

'I think Kitty is going to drown herself in our pool.'

'Oh dear,' Mitchell grimaced. 'Why's that?'

'I just get that impression.'

She did not want to say she had opened the envelope meant for her father. Mitchell switched the blender on and watched the chestnuts and sugar whirl into a paste and splatter over the palm trees on his shirt.

'If I threw you into the pool now you would float. Even I with my big stomach would float.'

He was shouting over the noise of the blender. Nina waited for him to turn it off so she could whisper.

'Yes. She's been collecting stones. I was with her on the beach when she was looking for them.' She explained how Kitty told her she was studying the drains in the pool and had said mental things like, 'You don't want to get hair caught in the plumbing.'

Mitchell looked at the fourteen-year-old fondly. He realised she was jealous of the attention her father had been paying Kitty and probably wanted the girl to drown.

'Cheer up, Nina. Have some sweet chestnut purée on a spoon. I'm going to mix it with chocolate.' He licked his fingers. 'And I'm going to save a little square for the rat tonight.'

She knew a terrible secret no one else knew. And there were other secrets too. Yesterday when she was sitting on the bed in Kitty's room helping her nudge out the seeds from her plants, a bird was singing in the garden. Kitty Finch had put her head in her hands and sobbed like there was no tomorrow.

She must speak to her father, but he was in Nice making his way to some Russian church even though he had told her that if she was ever tempted to believe in God she might be having a nervous breakdown. Something else worried her. It was the thing under the bed, but she didn't want to think about that because it was something to do with Mitchell and anyway now her mother was calling her to go horse-riding.

Ponyland

The ponies were drinking water from a tank in the shade. Flies crawled over their swollen bellies and short legs and into their brown eyes that always seemed wet. As Nina watched the woman who hired them out brush their tails, she decided she would have to tell her mother about Kitty's drowning poem, as she now called it. Kitty was speaking in French to the pony woman and didn't look like someone who was about to drown herself. She was wearing a short blue dress and there were small white feathers in her hair, as if her pillow had burst in the night.

'We have to follow the trail. There's an orange plastic bag tied to the branches of the trees. The woman says we have to follow the orange plastic and walk either side of the pony.'

Nina, who wanted to be alone with her mother, found herself forced to choose a grey pony with long scabby ears and pretend she was having a perfect childhood.

The little pony was not in the mood to be hired out for an hour. She stopped every two minutes to graze the grass and nuzzle her head against the bark of trees. Nina was impatient. She had important things on her mind, not least the stones she had collected with Kitty on the beach, because she thought they were in the poem. She had seen the words 'The Drowning Stones' underlined in the middle of the page.

She noticed her mother was suddenly taking notice of things. When Kitty pointed out trees and different kinds of grasses, Isabel asked her to repeat their names. Kitty was saying that certain types of insects needed to drink nectar in the heatwave. Did Isabel know that honey is just spit and nectar? When bees suck nectar they mix it with their saliva and store the mixture in their honey sacs. Then they throw up their honey sacs and start all over again. Kitty was talking as if they were one big happy family, all the while holding the rope between her thumb and finger. Nina sat in silence on the pony, staring moodily at the cracks of blue sky she could see through the trees. If she turned the sky upside down the pony would have to swim through clouds and vapour. The sky would be grass. Insects would run across the sky. The trail seemed to have disappeared, because there were no more orange plastic bags tied to the branches of trees. They had come out of the pine forest into a clearing near a café. The café was opposite a lake. Nina scanned the trees for bits of ripped orange plastic and knew they were lost, but Kitty didn't care. She was waving at someone, trying to get the attention of a woman sitting alone on the terrace outside the café.

'It's Dr Sheridan. Let's go and say hello.'

She walked the pony straight off what remained of the trail and led it up the three shallow concrete steps towards Madeleine Sheridan, who had taken off her spectacles and placed them on the white plastic table next to her book.

Nina found herself stranded on the pony as Kitty led her past the bemused waitress carrying a tray of Orangina to a family at a nearby table. The old woman seemed to have frozen on her chair at the moment she was about to put a cube of sugar into her cup of coffee. It was as if the sight of a slender young woman in a short blue dress, her red hair snaking down her back, leading a grey pony on to the terrace of a café was a vision that could only be glanced at sideways. No one felt able to intervene because they did not fully know what it was they were seeing. It reminded Nina of the day she watched an eclipse through a hole in coloured paper, careful not to be blinded by the sun.

'How are you, Doctor?'

Kitty pulled at the rope and gave the pony a sugar cube. With one hand still holding the rope, she draped her arm around the old woman's shoulder.

Madeleine Sheridan's voice when she finally spoke was calm, authoritative. She was wearing a red shawl that looked like a matador's cloak with pom-poms sewn across the edge.

'Stick to the track, Kitty. You can't bring ponies in here.'

'The track has disappeared. There's no track to stick to.' She smiled. 'I'm still waiting for you to bring me back my shoes like you said you would. The nurses told me I had dirty feet.'

Nina glanced at her mother, who was now standing on the left side of the pony. Kitty's hands were shaking and she was speaking too loudly.

'I'm surprised you haven't told my new friends what you did to me.' She turned to Isabel and imitated a horror-film whisper: 'Dr Sheridan said I have a morbid predisposition.'

To Nina's dismay, her mother actually laughed as if she and Kitty were sharing a joke.

The waitress brought out a plate of sausages and green

beans and thumped it in front of Madeleine Sheridan, muttering to her in French about getting the pony out of the café.

Kitty winked at Nina. First with her left eye. And then with her right eye. 'The waitress isn't used to ponies coming in for breakfast.'

On cue the pony started to lick the sausages on the plate and all the children at the next table laughed.

Kitty took a small sip of the doctor woman's untouched coffee. Her eyes had stopped winking. 'Actually ' – her knuckle suddenly turned white as she gripped the rope that was supposed to keep the pony on the trail – 'she had me locked up.' She wiped her mouth with the back of her hand. 'I EMBARRASSED HER SO SHE CALLED AN AMBULANCE.'

Kitty picked up the knife from the plate, a sharp knife, and waved it at Madeleine Sheridan's throat. All the children in the café screamed, including Nina. She heard the old woman, her voice straining, telling her mother that Kitty was sick and unpredictable. Kitty was shaking her head and shouting at her.

'You said you'd get my clothes. I waited for you. You're a LIAR. I thought you were kind but they electrocuted me because of you. They did it THREE times. The nurse wanted to shave off some of my HAIR.'

The point of her knife hovered a centimetre away from Madeleine Sheridan's milky pearl necklace.

'I want to go!' Nina shouted at her mother, trying to keep her balance as the pony, its pointed ears now alert, jerked forward to find the bowl of sugar cubes.

Isabel tried to undo the stirrups so Nina could get off

the pony. The waitress was helping her with the buckles and Nina managed to swing her legs over the saddle but didn't dare jump because the pony suddenly reared up.

Someone in the café was calling the park keeper on the telephone.

'THEY BURNED MY THOUGHTS TO MAKE THEM GO AWAY.'

As she moved closer to Madeleine Sheridan, waving the knife at her stricken frozen face, two small white feathers caught in her hair drifted towards Nina, who was still struggling to get off the pony.

'The doctors PEEPED at me through a spyhole. They forced MEAT down my throat. I tried to put on face cream but my jaws HURT from the shocks. I would rather DIE than have that done to me again.'

Nina heard herself speak.

'Kitty is going to drown herself.'

It was as if she was the only person who could hear her own voice. She was saying important things but apparently not important enough.

'Katherine is going to drown herself.'

Even to her own ears it sounded like a whisper, but she thought the old woman doctor might have heard her all the same. Her mother had somehow managed to grab the knife out of Kitty's hand and Nina heard Madeleine Sheridan's wobbling voice say, 'I must telephone the police. I'm going to call her mother. I must call her straight away.' She stopped because Jurgen had suddenly arrived.

It was as if Kitty had conjured him in her mind. He was

talking to the park keeper, who was shaking his head and looked flustered.

'I have witnesses.' The pom-poms on Madeleine Sheridan's red cape were jumping up and down as if they were the witnesses she referred to.

Kitty grabbed Jurgen's arm and hung on to him. 'Don't listen to Dr Sheridan. She's obsessed with me. I don't know why but she is. Ask Jurgen.'

Jurgen's sleepy eyes blinked behind his round spectacles.

'Come on, Kitty Ket, I'll take you home.' He said something to Madeleine Sheridan in French and then put his arm around Kitty's waist. They could hear his voice soothing her. 'Forget forget Kitty Ket. We are all of us sick from pollution. We must take a nature cure.'

Madeleine Sheridan's eyes were burning like coal. Blue coal. She wanted to call the police. It was an attack. An assault. She looked like a matador that had been gored by the bull. The park keeper fiddled with a ring of keys strapped to his belt. The keys were almost as big as he was. He wanted to know where the young woman lived. What was her address? If Madame wanted him to call the police they would need this information. Isabel explained that Kitty had arrived five days ago with nowhere to stay and they had given her a room in their rented villa.

He frowned over this information, tapping his keys with his tiny thumb. 'But you must have asked her questions?'

Isabel nodded. They had asked her questions. Jozef

asked her what a leaf was. And a cotyledon.

'I don't think we need bother the police. It's a private argument. Madame is shaken but not harmed.'

Her voice was gentle and a little bit Welsh.

The keeper was gesticulating now. 'The young woman must have come from somewhere.' He paused to nod to two men in muddy boots who seemed to need his permission to cut through a log with a circular saw.

'Yes,' Madeleine Sheridan snapped, 'she came from a hospital in Kent, Great Britain.' She tapped the assaulted pearls tied in a knot near her throat and turned to Isabel Jacobs. 'I believe your husband is taking her out for a cocktail at the Negresco tomorrow.'

FRIDAY

On the Way to Where?

People stopped to look at her. To gaze and gaze again at the vision of a radiant young woman in a green silk dress who seemed to be walking on air. The left strap of her white tap-dancing shoes had come undone, as if to help lift her above the cigarette butts and chocolate wrappers on the paving stones. Kitty Finch with her wealth of hair piled on top of her head was almost as tall as Joe Jacobs. As they strolled down the Promenade des Anglais in the silver light of the late afternoon, it was snowing seagulls on every rooftop in Nice. She had casually slung the short white feather cape across her shoulders, its satin ribbons tied in a loose knot round her neck. The feathers fluttered in the wind blowing from the sea, the Mediterranean, which, Joe mused, was the same colour as the glittery blue kohl on her eyes.

In the distance they could see the pink dome of the Hotel Negresco. He had respectfully changed into a pinstriped suit and even opened the new bottle of perfume sent to him from

Zurich. His parfumier, the last alchemist living in the twentieth century, insisted the top notes were irrelevant and the deepest notes would present when he was perspiring. Kitty slipped her bare arm through his pinstriped arm, a vertical red stripe that was not unlike the centipede he had caught in the river. She did not tell him what had happened with Madeleine Sheridan (she and Jurgen had already discussed it for hours) and he did not tell her how he had found himself on his knees lighting one and then two candles at the Russian Orthodox Cathedral. The tension of waiting to meet each other again had made them do things they did not understand.

By the time they arrived at the marble entrance, the porter in his crimson jacket and white gloves respectfully swung open the door for them, NEGRESCO printed across the arch of glass in gold letters. Her feather cape flew behind her like the wings of the swan they were plucked off. She did not so much stroll as glide into the low-lit bar with its faded red velvet armchairs and tapestries on the walls.

'See those oil paintings of noblemen in their palace?'

He looked up at the portraits of what appeared to be solemn pale aristocrats posing on chairs covered in tapestry in chilly marble rooms.

'Yeah, well, my mother cleans their silver and washes their underpants.'

'Is she a cleaner?'

'Yeah. She used to clean the villa for Rita Dwighter. That's how I get to stay free sometimes.'

This confession made her blush but he had something to say in reply.

'My mother was a cleaner too. I used to steal hen's eggs for her and bring them home in my pockets.'

They sat side by side on two antique chairs. The white feathers of her cape trembled when he whispered, 'There's a note to us on the table. I think it must be from Marie Antoinette.'

Kitty reached over and picked up the white card propped against a vase of flowers.

'It says the cocktail of the month is champagne with something called Crème de Fraise des Bois.'

Joe nodded as if this information was of vital importance.

'After the revolution everyone shall have the cocktail of the month. Shall we have one now anyway?'

Kitty nodded enthusiastically.

The waiter was already at his side, taking his order as if it were a great privilege to do so. A bored musician in a stained white dinner jacket sat at the piano playing 'Eleanor Rigby' in the corner of the bar. She crossed her legs and waited for him to talk about her poem. Last night she saw something that scared her and she wanted to tell him about it. The boy was standing by her bed again. He was waving frantically like he was asking her to help him and he had two hen's eggs in his pocket. He had broken into her mind. She had started to cover mirrors in case he appeared again. She slipped her hands under the bag on her lap so he wouldn't see they were shaking.

'Tell me more about your mother. Does she look like you?'

'No, she's obese. You could make the whole of me from one of her arms.'

'You said she knows the owner of the villa?'

'Yeah. Rita Dwighter.'

'Say more about Rita and her portfolio of property and pain.'

She did not want to talk about her mother's boss. It was shrapnel in her arm, his indifference to the envelope she had pushed through his bedroom door. He kept changing the subject. She took a deep breath and smelt the clover in his perfume.

'Rita owns so much property she has become a tax exile in Spain, but that means she can only be in the UK for a certain number of days a year. My mother told her she'll be like someone on the run and Rita took offence and said her own shrink told her she must accept her greed.'

He laughed and sank his fingers into the small bowl of nuts on the table. They clinked glasses and took their first sip of the cocktail of the month.

'What is your favourite poem, Kitty?'

'Do you mean a poem I've written or someone else's?' He must know by now that he was her favourite poet. That was why she was here. His words were inside her. She understood them before she read them. But he wouldn't own up. He was always cheerful. So fucking cheerful, she thought he might be in terrible danger.

'I mean do you like Walt Whitman or Byron or Keats or Sylvia Plath?'

'Oh, right.' She took another sip of her cocktail. 'Well, there's no competition. My favourite poem is by Apollinaire.'

'What's that?'

She tipped her chair forward and grabbed the fountain

pen he always clipped on to his shirt like a microphone.

'Give me your hand.'

When he placed his hand on her knee, his palm making a sweaty mark on her green silk dress, she jabbed the nib into his skin so hard he jumped. She was stronger than she looked, because she held his hand down and he couldn't or didn't want to tear it away. She was hurting him with his own pen as she inked a black tattoo of letters on his skin.

I
T
S
R
A
I
N
I
N
G

He stared at his smarting hand. 'Why do you like it so much?'

She lifted the champagne flute up to her lips and stuck her tongue inside it, licking the last dregs of strawberry pulp.

'Because it's always raining.'

'Is it?'

'Yeah. You know it is.'

'Do I?'

'It's always raining if you're feeling sad.'

The image of Kitty Finch in perpetual rain, walking in rain, sleeping in rain, shopping and swimming and collecting plants in rain, intrigued him. His hand was still on her knee. She had not put the lid back on his pen. He wanted to demand she return it to him but instead found himself offering her another cocktail. She was lost in thought. Sitting up very straight on the velvet armchair with his pen in her hand. The gold nib pointing to the ceiling. Small diamonds of sweat dripped down her long neck. He walked to the bar and leaned his elbows against the counter. Perhaps he should beg the staff to drive him home? It was impossible. It was an impossible flirtation with catastrophe, but it had already happened, it was happening. It had happened and it was happening again, but he must fight it to the end. He stared at the black rain she had inked on his hand and told himself it was there to soften his resolve to fight. She was clever. She knew what rain does. It softens hard things. He could see her searching her bag for something. She had a book in her hand, one of his own books, and she was underlining something on the page with his pen. Perhaps she was an extraordinary writer? It hadn't occurred to him. Perhaps that is what she was?

Joe ordered two more cocktails of the month. The barman told Monsieur he'd bring them over when they were ready but he did not want to walk back to his antique armchair yet. She was really quite knowledgeable about poetry. For a botanist. Why had he not told her he had read her poem? What was stopping him? Should he trust his instinct not to reveal he had read the threat she had slipped into the envelope? He carried the iced flutes over to her. This time Joe glugged back his strawberry champagne as if it was a pint of pale ale. He bent towards her lips, which were wet from the strawberry champagne, and kissed her. When she let him, he kissed her again, his black silver hair tangling with the curls of her red hair. Her pale eyelashes sooty with mascara fluttered against his cheek while he held her long neck in the palm of his hand and felt her painted green fingernails press into his knee.

'We're kissing in the rain.' Her voice was hard and soft at the same time. Like the velvet armchairs. Like the black rain inked on his hand.

Her eyes were squeezed tight shut. He was walking her towards the heavy Austrian chandelier in the lobby. Her head was spinning and she needed some water. She could hear him asking the Italian receptionist if there were vacancies for rooms. She opened her eyes. The sleek Italian pressed his fingers on the keyboard of his computer. Yes, there was a room. But it was decorated in the style of Louis XVI rather than art deco and it did not have a sea view. Joe handed over his credit card. The bellhop led them into a lift lined with mirrors. He wore white gloves on his hands. He was pressing buttons. She stared at the multiple reflections of Joe's sweating arm around her waist, the green silk of her dress trembling as they sailed silently in the lift that smelt of leather to the third floor.

Metaphors

Madeleine Sheridan formally invited Isabel to Maison Rose. She gave her a glass of sherry and told her to make herself comfortable on the uncomfortable chaise longue. She sat herself down in the armchair opposite the journalist wife and delicately removed a few strands of silver hair from her glass of whisky. Her eyes were cloudy like the pool Kitty Finch had complained about to Jurgen and she thought she might be losing her sight. This made her all the more determined to help Isabel Jacobs see things clearly. To help her understand that being threatened with a knife was a serious business and strangely enough she experienced a sharp pain across her throat even though Kitty Finch had not in reality touched her throat. She was very much Dr Sheridan and not Madeleine when she explained that she had telephoned Kitty's mother, who would be arriving early on Sunday morning. Mrs Finch would drive from the airport to the villa to collect her daughter and take her home. Isabel stared at her sandals.

'You seem convinced she is very ill, Madeleine.'

'Yes. Of course she is.'

Every time Isabel spoke, Madeleine Sheridan reckoned it was as if she was reading the news. Her mission to help the exotic Jacobs family see things as they really are was on full alert.

'Life is something she has to do but she doesn't want to do it. Nina has told us as much.'

Isabel sipped her sherry.

'But Madeleine . . . it's only a poem.'

Dr Sheridan sighed. 'The girl has always been a bit of a mess. But what a beauty, eh?'

'She is very beautiful, yes.' Isabel heard herself say this sentence awkwardly, as if she were scared of it.

'If I may ask you, Isabel . . . why did you invite a stranger into your home?'

Isabel shrugged as if the answer was entirely obvious.

'She had nowhere to stay and we have more rooms than we need. I mean, who needs five bathrooms, Madeleine?'

Madeleine Sheridan tried to look straight through Isabel Jacobs but what she saw, she had to admit, was a blur. Her own lips were moving. She was speaking to herself in French because the things she was saying were less suited to the English language. Her thoughts were making a hard noise against her lips, Kah, Kah, Kah, as if she was indeed obsessed with Kitty Finch, who, for some reason, was so adored by Jurgen and everyone else she managed to manipulate and intrigue. For the last three weeks she had observed the Jacobs family from the best seat in the theatre, the hidden chair on her balcony. Isabel Jacobs might have pushed Kitty Finch into her ridiculous husband's arms, but it was a foolhardy thing to risk because she would lose her daughter. Yes. If her husband seduced the sick girl it would be impossible to return to life as it had been before. Isabel would have to ask her husband to leave the family house. Nina Jacobs, like an assassin, would have to choose which parent she could live without. Did Isabel not understand that her daughter had already adapted to life without her mother in it? Madeleine Sheridan tried to stop her lips from moving, because they said such unpleasant things. She could just about make out Isabel shifting on the chaise longue. Crossing her legs. Uncrossing her legs. The heat outside was so fierce she had switched on the ancient air-conditioning system. It groaned above her head. Madeleine could sense (although she could not see) that Isabel was a brave woman. When she was at medical school she had observed women train as heart specialists, gynaecologists, bone cancer consultants. Then they had children and something happened. They became tired. All the time. Madeleine Sheridan wanted this groomed, enigmatic woman sitting in her living room to fade, to be exhausted, to display some sort of vulnerability, to need her and above all to value this conversation.

Instead the betrayed wife rolled her long black hair in her fingers and asked for another sherry. She was almost flirtatious.

'When did you retire, Madeleine? I have often interviewed doctors working in the most difficult situations. No stretchers, no lights, sometimes no medication.'

Madeleine Sheridan's throat hurt. She leaned towards the woman she was trying to destroy, took a shallow breath and waited for the words to come, something about her work before she retired and the difficulty of persuading patients on low incomes to give up smoking.

'It's my birthday today.'

She heard the small begging voice that came out of her mouth but it was too late to try and catch another tone. If she could have said it again it would have been light, airy, amused at being alive at all. Isabel looked genuinely taken aback.

'Happy birthday! If you'd told me I would have bought a bottle of champagne.'

'Yes. Thank you for the thought.' Madeleine Sheridan heard herself speaking in entitled middle-class English again.

'Someone has burgled my garden. My roses have been stolen and of course I know that Kitty Finch is very angry with me.'

The exotic wife of the poet was saying something about how stealing a rose was not exactly proof of insanity and anyway it was getting late and she wanted to say goodnight to her daughter. From the window opposite she saw a full moon float across the sky. What was the poet's wife doing? She was walking towards her. She was getting closer. She could smell honey.

Isabel Jacobs was wishing her happy birthday again and her lips were warm on her cheek. The kiss hurt as much as the pains in her throat.

Foreign Languages

Nina was asleep but in her dream she was awake and she found herself walking towards the spare room where Kitty lay on the bed. Her face was swollen and her lip was split. She looked like Kitty but not a lot. She heard Kitty whisper her name.

Nina crept closer. Kitty's eyelids were dusted with green eyeshadow. They looked like leaves. Nina sat on the end of the bed. Kitty was forbidden because she was dangerous. She did dangerous things. Nina swallowed hard and gave dead Kitty some information.

Your mother is coming to get you.

She placed a blue sugar mouse on the edge of Kitty's foot. It had a tiny tail made from string. Nina had found it under Kitty's bed.

And I've bought you some soap.

She had seen Kitty look for soap lots of times but there wasn't any in her bathroom and she said she'd spent all her money on the hire car.

I read your poem. I think it's brilliant. It's the best thing I've ever read in my life.

She quoted Kitty's lines to her. Not like how they were in the poem but how she remembered them.

> Jumping forwards with both feet
> Jumping backwards with both feet
> Thinking of ways to live

Kitty's eyelids trembled and Nina knew she had got the poem all wrong and hadn't remembered it properly. And then she asked Kitty to stick out her tongue, but Kitty was speaking to her in Yiddish or it might have been German and she was saying, 'Get up!', which is what made Nina wake up.

Money is Hard

He slipped his hands around her neck and untied the white satin ribbon of her feather cape. The four-poster bed draped in heavy gold curtains resembled a cave. She heard a car alarm go off while seagulls screamed on the window ledge and her eyes were fixed on the wallpaper. The white feathers of her cape lay scattered on the sheet as if it had been attacked by a fox. She had bought it in a flea market in Athens but had never worn it until now. A swan was a symbol of the dying year in autumn, she had read that somewhere. It had stuck in her head and made her think of the way swans stick their heads in the water and turn themselves upside down. She had been saving the cape for something, perhaps for this; it was hard to know what she had had in mind when she exchanged money for the feathers that had insulated this water-bird from the cold and were also made from quills that were once used as pens. He was inside her now but he was inside her anyway, that was what she couldn't tell him but she had told him in her poem which he had not read and now the car alarm had stopped and she could hear voices outside the window. A thief must have broken into a car, because someone was sweeping up broken glass.

After a while he ran her a bath.

They walked down to reception and she stood under the blinding Austrian crystals of the chandelier while Joe signed something with his pen. The Italian receptionist gave him back his credit card and the porter opened the glass doors for them. Everything was like it was before but a little bit different. The pianist was still playing 'Eleanor Rigby' in the bar they had left two hours ago, except now he was singing the words. The palm trees planted along the two lanes of traffic were lit up with golden fairy lights. Kitty jangled the car keys in her hand and told Joe to wait while she bought herself a sugar mouse from the candy stall on the esplanade. The mice were lined up on a silver tray. Pink white yellow blue. She pushed in front of a Vietnamese woman buying strawberry marshmallows and examined the tiny tails made from string. She eventually chose a blue mouse, dropping the car keys as she searched her bag for coins. When they got to the car she told him she was hungry. Her stutter had returned to torment them both. Would he mind if she stopped somewhere for a pah pah pah? Of course, he said, I'd like a pizza too, and they found a restaurant with tables outside in the warm night next to a church. It was the first time he had seen her eat. She devoured the thin pizza with anchovies and he bought her another one with capers and they drank red wine as if they were indeed the lovers they were not supposed to be. She played with the night-lights burning on the table, making prints of her fingertips from the wax, and when he requested she give him one to keep for ever she told him her fingerprints were all over his body anyway. And then she told him about the hospital in Kent and how the nurses from Odessa compared their love bites in the lunch break. She had written about that too but she was not asking him to read it – she was just telling him it would be part of her first collection of poetry. He helped her to salad and spooned artichokes on to her plate and watched her long fingers mop up the oil with bread. They clinked glasses and she told him how after the shock treatment when she lay damaged on the white sheets she knew the English doctors had not erased the thoughts inside her head, etc, but he would know all about that and why go into it now because the night was soft here in the alleyways of old Nice in contrast to the day when it was hard and smelt of money. To all of this he nodded and though he asked her no questions he knew that in a way they were talking about her poem. Two hours later, when they were halfway up the mountain road, Kitty hunched over the steering wheel as she manoeuvred the car around perilous bends, he glanced at his watch. She was a skilled driver. He admired her firm hands with their waxy fingertips on the steering wheel as she pulled the car round the mountain bends. Kitty beeped the horn as a rabbit ran across the road and the car swerved.

She asked him to open his window so she could hear the animals calling to each other in the dark. He wound down the window and told her to keep her eyes on the road. 'Yes,' she said again, her eyes now back on the road. Her silk dress was falling off her shoulders as she bent over the steering wheel. He had something to ask her. A delicate request which he hoped she would understand.

'It would be better for Isabel if she does not know what happened tonight.'

Kitty laughed and the blue mouse bounced in her lap.

'Isabel already knows.'

'Knows what?' He told her he was feeling dizzy. Would she slow down?

'That's why she invited me to stay. She wants to leave you.'

He needed the car to move slowly. He had vertigo and could feel himself falling although he knew he was sitting in the passenger seat of a hire car. Was it true that Isabel had started the beginning of the end of their marriage and invited Kitty Finch to be the last betrayal? He dared not look down at the waterfalls roaring against the rocks or the up-rooted shrubs that clung to the sides of the mountain.

He heard himself say, 'Why don't you pack a rucksack and see the poppy fields in Pakistan like you said you wanted to?'

'Yes,' she said. 'Will you come with me?'

He lifted his arm that had been resting on her shoulders and gazed at the words she had written on his hand. He had been branded as cattle are branded to show whom they belong to. The cold mountain air stung his lips. She was driving too fast on this road that had once been a forest. Early humans had lived in it. They studied fire and the movement of the sun. They read the clouds and the moon and tried to understand the human mind. His father had tried to melt him into a Polish forest when he was five years old. He knew he must leave no trace or trail of his existence because he must never find his way home. That was what his father had told him. You cannot come home. This was not something possible to know but he had to know it all the same.

•

'Why haven't you read my pah pah pah?'

'My sweetheart' is what she heard him say as she pressed her white shoe on the brakes. The car lurched towards the edge of the mountain. His voice was truly tender when he said 'My sweetheart'. Something had changed in his voice. Her head was buzzing as if she had knocked back fifteen espressos one after the other. And then eaten twelve lumps of sugar. She turned the engine off, pulled the handbrake up and leaned back in her seat. At last. At last he was talking to her.

'It is dishonest to give me a poem and pretend to want my opinion when what you really want are reasons to live. Or reasons not to die.'

'You want reasons to live too.'

He leaned towards her and kissed her eyes. First the left and then the right, as if she was already a corpse.

'I'm not the right reader for your poem. You know that.'

She thought about this while she sucked on her blue mouse.

'The important thing is not the dying. It's making the decision to die that matters.'

He took out his handkerchief to hide his own eyes. He had vowed never to show the dread and worthlessness and panic in his own eyes to his wife and daughter. He loved them, his dark-haired wife and child, he loved them and he could never tell them what it was that had been on his mind for a long time. The unwelcome tears continued to pour out of him just as they had poured out of Kitty Finch in the orchard full of suffering trees and invisible growling dogs. He must apologise for not stamping on his own desires, for not fighting it all the way.

'I'm sorry about what happened in the Negresco.'

'What happened in the Negresco that you're sorry about?'

Her voice was soft, confident and reasonable.

'I know you like silk so I wore a silk dress.'

He felt her fingers tap his wet cheek and he could smell his perfume in her hair. To have been so intimate with her had brought him to the edge of something truthful and dangerous. To the edge of all the bridges he had stood on in European cities. The Thames flowing east across southern England and emptying into the North Sea. The Danube that started in the Black Forest of Germany and ended in the Black Sea. The Rhine that ended in the North Sea. Sex with her had brought him to the edge of the yellow line on the platforms of tube and train stations where he had stood thinking about it. Paddington. South Kensington. Waterloo. Once in the Metro in Paris. Twice in Berlin. Death had been on his mind for a long time. The thought, the throwing of himself into rivers and into trains lasted two seconds, a tremor, a twitch, a blink and a step forwards but, so far, a step backwards again. A step back to five beers for the price of four, back to roasting a chicken for Nina, back to tea, Yorkshire or Tetley's, never Earl Grey, back to Isabel, who was always somewhere else.

He was the wrong reader for her to ask if she should live or die because he was barely here himself. He wondered what kind of catastrophe lived inside Kitty Finch. She told him she had forgotten what she remembered. He wanted to close down like Mitchell and Laura's shop in Euston. Everything that was open must close. His eyes. His mouth. His nostrils. His ears that could still hear things. He told Kitty Finch he had read her poem and that it been ringing inside him ever since. She was a writer of immeasurable power and more than anything he hoped she would do the things she wanted to do. She must travel to the Great Wall in China, to the vitality and dream that is India, and she must not forget the mysterious luminous lakes closer to home in Cumbria. These were all things to look forward to.

It was getting dark and she told him the brakes on the hire car were fucked, she couldn't see a thing, she couldn't even see her hands.

He told her to keep her eyes on the road, to just do that, and while he was speaking she was kissing him and driving at the same time.

'I know what you're thinking. Life is only worth living because we hope it will get better and we'll all get home safely. But you tried and you did not get home safely. You did not get home at all. That is why I am here, Jozef. I have come to France to save you from your thoughts.'

SATURDAY

Nina Ekaterina

When Nina woke up just after dawn on Saturday morning she knew immediately everything had changed. The doors of her balcony were wide open as if someone had been there in the night. When she saw a yellow square of paper rolled up like a scroll on her pillow she knew she would be wiser to go back to sleep and hide all day. The words on the yellow paper were written in shaky handwriting by someone who was in a hurry and who obviously liked writing things down. She finished reading the note and crept downstairs to the French doors that led to the pool. They were already open, as she thought they would be. She knew what she was going to see.

Something was floating in the pool and that did not surprise her. At a second glance she saw that Kitty's body was not so much floating as submerged vertically in the water. She was wrapped in a tartan dressing gown but the gown had slipped. The yellow lilo bounced against the edges of the pool and floated towards the body. She heard herself call out.

'Kitty?'

The head was low in the water, tilted back with its mouth open. And then she saw the eyes. The eyes were glassy and open and they were not Kitty's eyes.

'Dad?'

Her father did not reply. She thought he was playing a joke on her. Any second he would rise from the water and roar at her.

'Dad?'

His body was so big and silent. All the noise that was her father, all the words and spluttering and utterances inside him, had disappeared into the water. All she knew was that she was screaming and then suddenly doors were banging and her mother had dived into the pool. Mitchell jumped in too. Together they steered the body around the lilo and with difficulty were trying to lift it out of the pool. Nina heard her mother shout something to Laura. She watched Mitchell lay the body down on the paving stones and press his hands up and down on it. She could hear the sound of water splashing as her mother heaved the dressing gown out of the water. She did not understand why it was so heavy but then she saw her mother pull something out of the pockets. It was a pebble the size of her hand and it had a hole in the middle of it. Nina could see her struggling with three more of the pebbles she had collected on the beach with Kitty and she thought it must have got later and the sun was rising over the pool because the water had changed colour. She shivered and searched for the sun in the sky but she could not see it.

Mitchell stuck his fingers in her father's mouth. And then he pinched his nose. Mitchell was panting and actually kissing her father over and over again.

'I don't know. I don't know.'

Laura ran into the villa shouting something about the fact sheet. Where was Jurgen? Everyone was shouting for Jurgen. Nina felt someone touch her head. Kitty Finch was stroking her hair. And then Kitty pushed her through the French doors and told her to sit down on the sofa while she helped Laura look for the fact sheet. That's all she heard for the next five minutes. Where was the fact sheet? Had anyone seen the fact sheet? Although Nina was still not sure whether it was her father or Kitty who was alive or dead she sat obediently on the sofa and stared at the Picasso prints on the wall. A fish bone. A blue vase. A lemon. It was only when she heard Laura shouting, 'It's yellow. The fact sheet is a yellow piece of paper,' that she realised she was holding a yellow sheet of paper in her hand and waved it at Laura. Laura looked startled and then grabbed it from her and ran to the telephone. Nina watched her peer at the numbers.

'I don't know, Kitty. I don't know which one to call.'

Kitty was saying something in a detached flat voice.

'The hospital is in Grasse on the Chemin de Clavary.'

It began to rain. Nina heard herself sobbing. She was standing outside herself looking at herself as she stood by the glass doors.

The ambulance and the police were arriving. Madeleine Sheridan was there too. She was shouting at Mitchell.

'Tilt his head upwards, hold his nose!' and Nina could see

her fingers press into her father's neck as she felt for a pulse.

'Do not put him in the recovery position, Mitchell. I think he has a spinal injury.'

And then she heard the old woman cry out, 'There it is . . .'

Nina started to sob in the rain because she was still not sure what had happened. As she ran towards her mother she heard that she was a very loud crier. It sounded a bit like laughing but it wasn't. Her teeth were showing and she could feel little jabs in her diaphragm. She was frowning and the more she cried the more she frowned. She could feel her mother holding her in her arms, stroking her neck. Her mother was wearing a nightdress and it was wet and cold and she smelt of expensive creams. As a child she had played a morbid game in which she dared herself to have to choose which one of her parents she would rather die. She had tormented herself with this game and now she buried her face in her mother's stomach because she knew she had betrayed her.

Its softness against her cheek made her cry all the more and she thought her mother knew what she thinking because she heard her whisper in her ear, her words barely there, like an autumn leaf turning in the wind, 'Never mind, never mind.'

Her father was being laid out on a stretcher. The police had started to drain the pool. Jurgen was there too. He had a broom in his hand and was energetically sweeping around the plant pots. He had even managed to put on navy overalls that made him look like a caretaker.

The News

Isabel walked towards the paramedics and took Jozef's hand in her own. At first she thought a row of ants was crawling in a military line towards his knuckles. And then she saw the fading black inked vowels and consonants running into each other.

I
T
S

R
A
I
N
I
N
G

She could hear the drone of the bees nearby and she heard herself insisting that what her husband required was an air ambulance, but what she was mostly saying was his name.

Jozef. Please Jozef. Jozef. Jozef please.

Why did he hack into his hand like that? Where did he do it and how could he bear it and what did it mean? She squeezed his fingers and asked him to explain himself. She promised that in turn she would explain herself. She would do that right now. She told him she would have liked to feel his love fall upon her like rain. That was the kind of rain she most longed for in their long unconventional marriage. The paramedics told her to get out of the way but she did not move because she had always got out of his way. Loving him had been the greatest risk in her life. The thing, the threat was lurking there in all his words. She had known that from the beginning. She had always known that. He had buried unexploded shells and grenades across the roads and tracks of all his books, they were under every poem, but if he died now her daughter would walk through a world that was always damaged and she was as angry as it was possible to be.

Jozef. Please Jozef. Jozef. Jozef. Please.

She suddenly understood that someone was pushing her out of the way and that she could smell blood.

A large man with a shaven head and a revolver strapped to his belt was asking her questions. To every question he asked she did not have a straightforward answer. What was her husband's name?

Jozef Nowogrodzki in his passport. Joe Harold Jacobs on all other ID. In fact she didn't think his name was Nowogrodzki but that was the name his parents had written in his passport anyway. Nor did she tell him her husband had many other names: JHJ, Joe, Jozef, the famous poet, the British poet, the arsehole poet, the Jewish poet, the atheist poet, the modernist poet, the post-Holocaust poet, the philandering poet. So where was Monsieur Nowogrodzki's place of birth? Poland. Łódź. 1937. Łódź in English is pronounced Wodge but she didn't know how to say it in French. His parents' names?

She wasn't sure how to spell them. Did he have brothers and sisters? Yes. No. He had a sister. Her name was Friga.

The inspector looked baffled. Isabel did what she did best.

She told him the news except it was a bit out of date. Her husband was five years old when he was smuggled into Britain in 1942, half starved and with forged documents. Three days after he arrived his mother and father were deported along with his two-year-old sister to the Chelmno death camp in western Poland. The inspector, who did not understand much English, put his hand up in front of his face as if he was stopping the traffic on a busy road. He told the wife of the Jewish poet that it was unfortunate the Germans occupied Poland in 1939 but he had to point out he was now engaged in a murder inquiry in the Alpes-Maritimes in 1994. Would she agree that Monsieur Nowogrodzki or was it Monsieur Jacobs had left his daughter a final note? Or was it a poem? Or was it evidence? Whatever it might be it was addressed to Nina Ekaterina. He slipped the yellow fact sheet into a plastic folder. On one side were instructions for how to work the dishwasher. On the other side were five lines written in black ink. These were apparently instructions for his daughter.

It was not yet six am but the whole village had already heard the news. When Claude arrived at the villa with a bag full of bread, Mitchell, who for once was not interested in a morsel, sent him away, his eyes still smarting from the chlorine in the cloudy water. The paramedics shouted instructions to each other and Isabel told Nina she would be in the ambulance too. They were going to put tubes up her father's nose and pump his stomach on the way to the hospital. The ambulance began its journey down the mountain road. Nina felt herself being led by Claude to Madeleine Sheridan's house, which was called Maison Rose even though it was painted blue. On the way she saw Jurgen with his arms around Kitty Finch and when she heard Mitchell shout, 'Piss off and don't come back,' everyone heard what Kitty said next. She was whispering but she might as well have been screaming, because what she said was the thing everyone knew anyway.

'He shot himself with one of your guns, Mitchell.'

Mitchell's big body was bent over double. Something was happening to his eyes, nostrils, mouth. Tears and snot and saliva were pouring out of the holes in his face. Without a shot being fired his face had five holes in it. Holes for breathing, looking, eating. Everyone was gazing in his direction but what he saw was a blur. They were a mob full of holes just like him. How was he going to protect himself from the mob when they pointed the finger? He would tell the police the truth. When the ebony Persian weapon disappeared, he thought the mental girl had stolen it to punish him for hunting animals. The telephone was ringing and then it stopped ringing and he could hear Laura wailing. His muscles ached from dragging the body out of the water. It was so heavy. It was as heavy as a bear.

NINA JACOBS

London, 2011

Whenever I dream my twentieth-century dream about my father, I wake up and immediately forget my passwords for EasyJet and Amazon. It is as if they have disappeared from my head into his head and somewhere in the twenty-first century he is sitting with me on a bus crossing London Bridge watching the rain fall on the chimney of Tate Modern. The conversations I have with him do not belong to this century at all, but all the same I ask him why he never really told me about his childhood? He replies that he hopes my own childhood wasn't too bad and do I remember the kittens?

Our family kittens (Agnieska and Alicja) always smelt a bit feral and my childhood pleasure was to groom them with my father's hairbrush. They lay on my lap and I combed out their fur while they purred and patted my hand with their soft paws. When I got near their bottoms the fur was stuck together and tangled because they were still too young to lick themselves clean. Sometimes I left the fur balls on the sofa and my father pretended to swallow them. He'd open his mouth very wide and make out he'd gulped one down and that it was stuck in his throat and he was choking. My father spent his life trying to work out why people had frogs in their throat, butterflies in their stomach, pins and needles in their legs, a thorn in their side, a chip on their shoulder and indeed if they had coughed up fur balls he would have studied them too.

No, he says. I would not have studied the fur balls.

We agree that he and I learned to muddle along together. He washed my vests and tights and T-shirts, sewed buttons on my cardigans, searched for missing socks and insisted I should never be afraid of people talking to themselves on buses.

Yes, my father says. That's what you are doing now.

No, I reply, that's not what I am doing now. I am not saying what I'm thinking out loud. That would be mad. No one on this bus can hear me talking to you.

Yes, he says, but it wouldn't matter anyway because everybody's talking out loud on their phones.

I still have the beach towel he bought me in a souvenir shop in Nice. The words *Côte d'Azur Nice Baie des Anges* fly across a big blue sky in a sunny yellow font. Tourists on the beach are rendered in black dots and just behind it is a road lined with palm trees. On the right is the pink dome of the Hotel Negresco with a French flag flying into the towelly blue sky. What it's missing is Kitty Finch with her copper hair rippling down her waist waiting for my father to read her poem. If she was named after a bird it's possible she was making a strange call, perhaps an emergency call to my father, but I cannot think about her, or the pebbles we collected together, without wanting to fall through their holes out of the world. So I will replace her with my father walking through France's fifth biggest city on his way past its monuments and statues to buy a wedge of honeycomb for my mother. The year is 1994 but my father (who has an ice cream in his hand and not a phone) is having a conversation with himself and it's probably something sad and serious to do with the past. I have never got a grip on when the past begins or where it ends, but if cities map the past with statues made from bronze forever frozen in one dignified position, as much as I try to make the past keep still and mind its manners, it moves and murmurs with me through every day.

The next time I'm sitting on a bus crossing London Bridge and the rain is falling on the chimney of Tate Modern I must tell my father that when I read biographies of famous people, I only get interested when they escape from their family and spend the rest of their life getting over them. That is why when I kiss my daughter goodnight and wish her sweet dreams, she understands my wish for her is kind, but she knows, as all children do, that it's impossible to be told by our parents what our dreams are supposed to be like. They know they have to dream themselves out of life and back into it, because life must always win us back. All the same, I always say it.

I say it every night, especially when it rains.

AFTERWORD

Entering the Whirlpool:
commerce, politics, marriage and hearth

If, as a young aspirant writer in the early to mid 1990s, you raised your head and took a look around the British literary landscape, one figure stood out from all the others: Deborah Levy. Read two pages of her work, and it was instantly apparent that she was a writer as much at home within the fields of visual and conceptual art, philosophy and performance as within that of the printed word. She'd read her Lacan and Deleuze, her Barthes, Marguerite Duras, Gertrude Stein, and Ballard, not to mention Kafka and Robbe-Grillet – and was putting all these characters to work in new, exhilarating ways. Like the emotional and cerebral choreographies of Pina Bausch, her fiction seemed less concerned about the stories it narrated than about the interzone (to borrow Burroughs's term) it set up in which desire and speculation, fantasy and symbols circulated. Even commonplace objects took on eerie, intense dimensions, like Duchampian readymades or objects in dreams for Freud.

So And Other Stories couldn't have landed a bigger catch to kick off their first year of publishing. If the setting and plot of *Swimming Home* are borrowed, almost ironically, from the staid English-middle-class-on-holiday novel, all similarities end there. The book's real drama plays out through blue sugar mice who scuttle from candy stalls into nightmares; or stones with holes in that turn into voyeuristic (or myopic) telescopes, then lethal weights, then, simply, holes. What holds this kaleidoscopic narrative together, even as it tears its characters apart, is – in classical Freudian fashion – desire: desire and its inseparable flip side, the death drive. This comes embodied – nakedly, almost primordially, floating in the water to which it will return – in the figure of Kitty Finch, half doomed and daddy-obsessed Sylvia Plath, half post-breakdown Edie Sedgwick out of *Ciao! Manhattan*: volatile, imploding around a swimming pool. Lured towards her, and the vortex or whirlpool she mermaids at the side of, are the worlds of commerce, politics, marriage and hearth, and literature itself, as represented by two exotica traders, a war correspondent and a celebrated poet, all uneasily coupled. And, at the spectrum's far end, the teenage girl who will emerge as the novel's real protagonist, inheritor of its historical traumas.

Tom McCarthy
June 2011

Dear readers,

With the right book we can all travel far. And yet British publishing is, with illustrious exceptions, often unwilling to risk telling these other stories.

Subscriptions from readers make our books possible. They also help us approach booksellers, because we can demonstrate that our books already have readers and fans. And they give us the security to publish in line with our values, which are collaborative, imaginative and 'shamelessly literary' (Stuart Evers, *Guardian*).

All subscribers to our upcoming titles
• are thanked by name in the books
• receive a numbered, first edition copy of each book (limited to 300 copies for our 2011 titles)
• are warmly invited to contribute to our plans and choice of future books

Subscriptions are:
£20 – 2 books (two books per year)
£35 – 4 books (four books per year)

To find out more about subscribing, and rates for outside Europe, please visit: http://www.andotherstories.org/subscribe/

Thank you!

To find out about upcoming events and reading groups (our foreign-language reading groups help us choose books to publish, for example) you can
• join the mailing list at: www.andotherstories.org
• follow us on twitter: @andothertweets
• join us on Facebook: And Other Stories

This book was made possible by our advance subscribers' support – thank you so much!

Our Subscribers

Aca Szabo
Alexandra Cox
Ali Smith
Alisa Holland
Alison Hughes
Amanda Jones
Amanda Hopkinson
Ana Amália Alves da Silva
Ana María Correa
Anca Fronescu
Andrea Reinacher
Andrew Tobler
Andrew Blackman
Angela Kershaw
Anna Milsom
Anne Christie
Anne Withers
Anne Jackson
Barbara Glen
Bárbara Freitas
Briallen Hopper
Bruce Millar
Carlos Tamm
Carol O'Sullivan
Caroline Rigby
Catherine Mansfield
Cecilia Rossi
Charles Boyle
Charlotte Ryland
Christina MacSweeney
Claire Williams
Clare Horackova
Daniel Hahn
Daniel Gallimore
David Wardrop
Debbie Pinfold
Denis Stillewagt
Elena Cordan

Emma Staniland
Eric Dickens
Eva Tobler-Zumstein
Fiona Quinn
Fiona Miles
Gary Debus
Genevra Richardson
Georgia Panteli
Geraldine Brodie
Hannes Heise
Helen Leichauer
Helen Weir
Henriette Heise
Henrike Lähnemann
Iain Robinson
Ian Goldsack
Jennifer Higgins
Jimmy Lo
Jo Luloff
John Clulow
Jonathan Ruppin
Jonathan Evans
Joy Tobler
Judy Garton-Sprenger
Julia Sanches
Juro Janik
K L Ee
Kate Griffin
Kate Pullinger
Kate Wild
Kevin Brockmeier
Krystalli Glyniadakis
Laura Watkinson
Laura McGloughlin
Liz Tunnicliffe
Lorna Bleach
Louise Rogers
Maisie Fitzpatrick

Margaret Jull Costa
Marion Cole
Nichola Smalley
Nick Stevens
Nick Sidwell
Nicola Hearn
Nicola Harper
Olivia Heal
Peter Law
Peter Blackstock
Philip Leichauer
Polly McLean
Rachel McNicholl
Rebecca Whiteley
Rebecca Miles
Rebecca Carter
Rebecca K. Morrison
Réjane Collard
Ros Schwartz
Ruth Martin
Samantha Schnee
Samantha Christie
Samuel Willcocks
Sophie Moreau
  Langlais
Sophie Leighton
Sorcha McDonagh
Steph Morris
Susana Medina
Tamsin Ballard
Tania Hershman
Tim Warren
Tomoko Yokoshima
Verena Weigert
Vivien Kogut Lessa
  de Sa
Will Buck
Xose de Toro